Billionaire Undaunted

THE BILLIONAIRE'S OBESSION
Zane

J. S. SCOTT

Billionaire Undaunted

Editing by Faith Williams – The Atwater Group
Proofread by Alicia Carmical – AVC Proofreading
Cover Artist: lorijacksondesign.com

ISBN: 978-1-939962-66-9 (Print)
ISBN: 978-1-939962-58-4 (E-Book)

Contents

Prologue

Seven months ago...

"Oh, dear God. This can't be possible. Not my sweet Chloe," Ellie Winters said to herself in a low, urgent whisper. She was alone in the doctor's office where she worked, so not a single soul heard the torment in her raspy voice. She was horrified by the videos she'd just seen on James's laptop computer—completely by accident—as she'd searched for a file her physician boss had requested.

It was a medical document she'd initially been searching for, something he'd asked her to print out for him. She'd gotten distracted when she saw an icon marked "Chloe's Videos," and she hadn't been able to resist looking at what she'd assumed were cheerful images of her best friend, even though she knew she was clicking into something she probably shouldn't.

She'd expected to see some happy snippets of her friend, a smiling Chloe that Ellie, quite frankly, hadn't seen in a while. Her buddy had been distracted and uncommonly nervous lately, and Ellie wished she knew the reason why. Chloe Colter was one of those people who was naturally kind and sweet.

Unfortunately, the scenes hadn't been joyous; the videos had been terrifying.

Ellie had only worked for Chloe's physician fiancé for a week or so, and he was demanding, but what she'd just seen made her realize that James was so much more than just a jerk.

He was pure evil!

Tears poured down Ellie's face as she signed out of the laptop and unplugged it, knowing she needed to get to Chloe as quickly as possible.

I have to talk to her. She can't marry him. Why in the hell is she even still engaged to him? The bastard should be in jail!

Dammit! Ellie was angry with herself that she hadn't dug deeper into *why* Chloe seemed so different since she'd returned to Rocky Springs. She'd assumed her friend was just distracted and adjusting to being home again after being away for so long to become an equine veterinarian. Or maybe she was stressed about her upcoming marriage to James. Getting married and planning a wedding *was* stressful, right? Especially when Chloe was still trying to establish her career.

There's a hell of a lot more to this story that I don't understand. I have to talk to Chloe, find out why she's hiding the fact that James is an abuser.

A fierce protectiveness fluttered in Ellie's stomach, as she remembered all the times Chloe had jumped to her defense in their twenty-something years of friendship. How many times had Chloe offered to help her out of her impoverished situation when they were kids? Ellie had lost count; just like she couldn't remember the number of times that Chloe's family had fed her when her mom had to work, or gave her new shoes or clothes to wear, Chloe claiming they didn't fit and wanted Ellie to have them.

So many sweet things Chloe and her mom have done for me over the years.

Choking back a sob of sadness, Ellie was determined to make sure her best friend didn't end up with the devil himself for a husband. Chloe deserved the most amazing husband in existence.

Why? Why is she covering for what James is doing to her?

Ellie didn't have the answers, but she was damn well going to find out. If need be, she'd drag Chloe out of the relationship kicking and screaming before she'd sit by and watch as the maid of honor while her friend got a life sentence with Satan.

Frantically, she gathered up her purse, ready to head out to Chloe's place. Ellie considered calling her, but she needed to confront her in person. She had no doubt that Chloe knew nothing about the videos, and would probably be horrified when she saw them.

Chloe Colter had been her best friend since grade school, and Ellie knew Chloe's terrified screams of pain and agony in the video weren't some kind of kinky sex game. Chloe had been traumatized, frightened, and begging for James to stop.

But the asshole never had. What kind of sick games was he playing, and how had Chloe ever gotten involved? Why hadn't she just walked away from him? After all, she was a Colter, and she didn't *need* any man. Chloe was rich and highly educated enough to lead her own life, and she had four older brothers who would have kicked the shit out of James had they realized what he'd done to her. Then there was the biggest question: why hadn't Chloe called the police on his ass? There *had* to be an explanation, but reason escaped Ellie in her rush to get out of the office.

The sound of someone jiggling the handle of the locked front door of the office made Ellie panic, and she gathered up the computer close to her body and sprinted from behind the desk, her heart racing as the door began to open.

She didn't look to see who was coming in. There were only a few people with a key, and she was one of them. Even if it was the cleaning crew, she wasn't about to chance waiting to find out. The only thing she could think of was sprinting for the back door, getting to her vehicle, and hightailing it straight to Chloe.

"Ellie!"

Hearing James's bellow from the reception area tripled her heart rate, and she flat-out ran for the back exit.

I just need to get to my car. I just need to get to Chloe.

Ellie could hear James's heavy steps pounding down the hallway behind her, but she kept on running, her breathing ragged from panic as she punched down the bar of the back exit and flew through the metal door without hesitation.

Hating herself for putting on heels that morning, she kept on sprinting as fast as her shoes would allow, clutching the laptop to her body like her life depended on it.

I have to get to Chloe. I have to get to Chloe. Please, just let me get to her place.

She'd almost made it to her beat-up little economy car—a vehicle she'd long ago dubbed the *Blue Turtle* because even though it was slow, it kept on moving—when James's body collided with hers. They both went to the ground, but unfortunately his body had her pinned to the cold concrete.

"Get. Off. Me." Her voice was a breathless hiss as she struggled to get out from under him.

"Is there some reason you're running away with my laptop, Ms. Winters?" James asked as he wrapped an arm around her neck.

"I'm going to work from home tonight." It was a lame excuse, but it was all Ellie could think of, and Chloe had always said she was a terrible liar. No matter what she claimed, she doubted James would believe it since she'd been running away from *him*, and he'd only asked her to find and print one document.

"You saw the videos," he accused menacingly. "You were going straight to Chloe. Nosy bitch. I asked you to do one thing on the computer and you just had to look at things that weren't intended to be seen by you or anyone else. Not now. You'll ruin everything. I'm glad I came back when I realized you might not mind your own business."

You shouldn't leave stuff you don't want seen on a computer that's accessible to anyone except you, dumbass.

Ellie was a crime show addict, and it was obvious that James was either sloppy or psychotic enough to not think about the possibility of her seeing it earlier. Feeling his arm tightening around her neck, she was pretty sure it was mostly the latter.

"Why are you trying to hurt Chloe?" Ellie gave up her pretense in her quest for answers. "She'd never do something like that to you. She loves you." The fact that Chloe had even cared about a monster like James made Ellie's stomach heave. The bastard had never deserved to even be in the same room as Chloe.

"Of course she loves me," James grunted. "We're getting married, and nobody is going to stop me. I'll finally get what I deserve."

Ellie wished he'd get what he *really* deserved: handcuffs and a very uncomfortable jail cell for the rest of his life. It was obvious that James thought he was entitled to Chloe's share of the Colter family fortune, a wealth that was almost unfathomable.

"You deserve to be in jail," Ellie gasped out with what little air she could suck in.

"Shut the fuck up! We're going to get up. I have a gun, and if you make a single noise, I'll fucking kill you," he rasped dangerously.

There was no question in Ellie's mind that James would follow through with his threat. After seeing how he'd treated Chloe, she had no doubt he was capable of just about anything.

He yanked her to her feet, and it didn't take long for her to see the glint of steel in the dim lights of the empty parking lot. He definitely had a weapon, and was prepared to use it. She considered screeching as loudly as possible, but she doubted it would do anything except get her silenced permanently. The office sat off by itself, down a dead end side street. It was after dark, and it was cold. The possibility of anybody hearing her was pretty slim. She decided if she didn't want to end up dead, she needed to wait until she could make her escape.

What happened next screwed up her plan.

"I told Chloe you were worthless. You have no value to her. Your family is poor, and you're poor. I only hired you to shut her up!" James exclaimed dangerously, right before he brought back his arm and punched her in the face.

Pain shot through Ellie's head as she absorbed the hit. Dazed from the brutal blow, she was incapable of resisting as he led her to his car parked on the other side of the parking lot.

As he slammed her against his vehicle, she finally spoke, desperately wondering if he was going to kill her even though she hadn't screamed. "James, you don't want to do this. What about Chloe? What about your career? Stop this now and I won't say anything. Just let me go home." She began to lie her ass off to get him to let her go.

"You think I'm stupid enough to believe that?" James asked in a voice that was growing high in pitch, a crazy voice that was beginning to scare Ellie half to death.

He's going to kill me.

Ellie recognized the loss of sanity in his tone.

He yanked the computer and her purse away from her and tossed both in the back seat of his vehicle before shoving her toward the trunk. The minute she heard the latch pop open, Ellie started to fight for her life.

No more trying to reason with James.

No more begging him to let her go.

She fought him with everything she had, trying to scratch at his eyes, kicking her leg up to catch him in the groin. He overpowered her, and she finally began to scream, knowing if he succeeded in getting her into the trunk of his vehicle, she was going to be a dead woman.

"Shut the fuck up," he growled menacingly, grasping her long blonde ponytail and yanking it so hard Ellie's eyes teared.

She didn't stop fighting even as he lifted her up and bodily tried to toss her into the confined space.

I'll be damned if I'll make this easy for him.

Her ass landed on the hard trunk surface, but she threw her arms out, trying to keep him from closing the lid, confining her in a makeshift coffin.

He'll never let me live.

"Nooooo! Somebody help! Please!" Ellie kept screaming, not caring anymore about James's warning, but nobody came to her rescue.

One more vicious slam to her head from his fist silenced her, made her world go dark.

With Ellie unconscious and incapable of fighting anymore, James closed the trunk and got into his vehicle, driving away into the night with her now-limp body hidden and confined in darkness.

Chapter 1

The Present...

"Where in the hell is she?" Zane Colter mumbled angrily as he drove his Bentley SUV up another steep, off-road track of dirt that would lead to *yet another* cabin in the desolate mountains.

How many days had he been searching? One day had rolled into the next, but Zane had been so laser-focused on his mission that he really hadn't bothered to do much else except stay hydrated.

He was grateful that he'd bought the new SUV just a month or two earlier. It was snowing hard here at high altitude, and his speed had been beyond reckless on the slick mountain roads. He knew he was driving too fast for the rapidly worsening weather conditions. Problem was, he *was* getting desperate. He knew which area Ellie was in because of the soil samples he'd taken from an old pair of James's shoes, and then from the tire treads from a late-model truck in his garage. After he'd found a tiny piece of a wilted, rare flower in the asshole's house, on a hunch, he'd taken those dirt samples, an intuition that had paid off after some intense analysis, pinpointing the only areas where that type of flower could grow and the soil it needed to thrive. The dirt he'd gathered had confirmed his suspicions. He was doubtful that James drove that older truck for anything other than mountain travel. The shoes were old and tattered, and a superficial asshole like James wouldn't wear them except in muddy areas where he wouldn't be seen. After matching the soil to the wilted flower, Zane had a very good idea of the area Ellie could be hidden. But a search of cabins and properties in the vicinity had brought up nothing that James owned, so Zane had to assume it was a place that wasn't titled under his real name.

"Where the fuck did he hide her? God dammit!" he growled as he slammed his hand against the steering wheel in frustration, knowing he was running out of time. Chances were he might be recovering a body instead of rescuing Ellie.

Not. Happening.

He shook off the possibility that Ellie could be dead and kept heading up to a small cabin a little bit farther up the nearly nonexistent dirt road he was currently climbing.

Wiping the sweat from his forehead with his hand and jamming his fingers through his hair in irritation, he deftly steered out of a spin on the ice and snow one-handed until he was climbing up the steep road again.

Pretty soon I'm going to have to face it; I've checked almost every cabin and home in this area with no fucking luck.

Zane had no idea how long it had been since he'd slept. He'd been doing research on the soil he'd found, and then working on pinpointing areas to investigate. He was exhausted, but a clock was ticking in his head, and if James *had* kept Ellie alive, she was probably running out of food and water. James was dead, and had been incapacitated before he'd offed himself. She'd been alone for too damn long.

I can't stop looking. I promised Chloe I wouldn't. I won't stop until I find her.

He shook his head absently, knowing that was a good excuse as to why he was out here searching, but his dogged persistence wasn't all about Ellie being his little sister's best friend. Instinct was gnawing at his gut, and it hadn't stopped.

He understood Ellie well enough to know that if she'd been able to get away, she would have. Some people claimed that Ellie was quiet, but he'd seen how bossy she could be when they were kids. As a teenager, she hadn't changed. She'd never had a problem voicing her opinions. Not with him.

Honestly, he'd never minded her anally retentive desire to organize. In fact, he'd kind of liked it since he wasn't exactly orderly in his personal life. Never had been. When it came to his work as a scientist, he was meticulous, but everything else went to hell outside of his lab. Truthfully, he'd always been fascinated by the way Ellie was able to juggle so many things at one time, and take care of them all in a hyper-organized way. She'd always been that way, even as an adolescent.

Zane could admit to himself that he'd liked Ellie in high school. But being his little sister Chloe's best friend had put Ellie completely off-limits for anything other than friendship after they had become adults. In high school, she'd been too young, too closely connected to his family. Not to mention the fact that he'd been so socially awkward in high school that he never would have had the balls to ask her out on a date, even if she hadn't been too young. But he'd liked her as a friend, too, and he still had fond feelings for her, even though he'd seen very little of her after he'd graduated from high school. He'd gone off to college, and had never come back home to live in Rocky Springs full-time.

He groaned as he pulled up to the cabin he'd been seeking. "Shit! It looks like a seasonal place."

Although the dwelling was in decent shape, it wasn't something a physician would own. It was tiny, and looked more like a hunting or fishing cabin.

Snow was drifted against the door, and it didn't look like anyone had been here since the first snow had flown. The white flakes were blowing and coming down in epic amounts as he jumped out of his vehicle, not bothering to lock it. Hell, nobody was coming up to this off-road cabin in the middle of a blizzard.

He trudged through the drifting snow and then kicked the accumulated white stuff from the front door as he turned the handle to enter, finding it locked. Annoyed and determined not to leave a single stone unturned, he put his shoulder against the door until the flimsy lock gave and then pushed it open.

"Ellie!" he bellowed loudly, even though the place was so small he probably didn't need to shout.

He strode through the small cabin with a living area to one side and a small kitchen in the other direction. He inspected the tiny bathroom before he came to an abrupt halt at the door of the only bedroom in the cabin. His body tensed as he saw the nearly unrecognizable figure shackled in the corner, huddled in a fetal position, completely naked.

"Fuck!" The curse exploded from his mouth as he entered the room and crouched down next to the woman, not knowing if she was dead or alive.

He pushed the filthy hair from her face. "Ellie?" he said hesitantly, feeling her neck for a pulse, his blood starting to boil as he saw all of the poorly healing bruises and cuts to her body, face, and limbs.

There was a portable potty next to her, but she'd obviously eventually lacked the strength to use it. Every limb was shackled with heavy metal, giving her very limited mobility. There was an empty water jug in the corner, and a plastic bag with nothing inside.

Zane got no response, but his heart started to accelerate as he found a weak pulse.

He ran out to the kitchen and found a glass and filled it with water, damn grateful that the place had indoor plumbing.

He paid no attention to how badly the woman smelled as he cradled her in his arms, forcing her to sit up. "Ellie? Open your eyes for me. You need water. You're dehydrated."

She was more than just dehydrated. She was starved. But he had to solve one problem at a time. Ellie used to be a curvy woman. Now she had no flesh on her bones.

He put the cup to her lips, tipping it up slowly. Her eyes flickered, but didn't open, and he hoped to hell she still had a swallow reflex. The last thing he wanted was for her to aspirate.

"Swallow for me, Ellie. Come on!" He watched her as he dribbled the water slowly into her mouth, relieved when he saw the muscles in her neck move weakly to down the liquid.

She needed food, but he continued to try to hydrate her first before finally going into the kitchen to try to find something—anything—that she might be able to get down her throat. Before he started rummaging through the cupboards, he remembered that he had protein drinks and some beverages in his SUV that would help her replace electrolytes she was missing.

"Fluids are better," he said absently to himself as he came back into the cabin with the supplies and tools he needed, then started his mission to get some more hydration and nutrition into Ellie.

He had to go slow, which irritated the hell out of him. He wanted to give her everything she hadn't had, and he wanted her nearly lifeless form to spring back to life.

He wanted Ellie back, and no matter what it took, he'd see her smiling and whole again if it killed him.

I won't quit. I never quit.

It took him a while to get her free from her bonds of steel with the tools he had in his car, and he continued to curse violently as he freed her.

If James wasn't already dead, Zane would have murdered the bastard without an ounce of remorse.

After he'd given Ellie everything he dared give her at one time, he scooped her up from the cold floor. *Christ!* She was so light that it scared the hell out of him. Ducking around the corner, he went into the bathroom, hoping the hot water worked. He turned the knobs on the shower, relieved when warm water eventually emerged.

Setting her gently on the floor, he quickly stripped off his own clothing and hefted her back up and into the shower with him. The cabin had some heat, but it was still damn cold. Ellie had no meat on her bones to protect her from lying on a cold floor. He needed to start off easy and gentle, increasing the warmth to her body carefully.

He used a bottle of liquid soap he'd found in the shower, scrubbing her body and hair until she was clean again. A small, weak moan escaped her lips, and it gave him even more hope that she'd come around eventually. She shivered in his arms, another good sign. His slow warming of her body was starting to bring up her core temperature.

Frustrated, Zane knew there was no way he was getting her to a medical facility because of the blizzard roaring outside the cabin walls. If something happened on the way back out of the remote wilderness, she'd never survive. He was a doctor. Granted, he was in research, but it wasn't like he hadn't gone to med school. Since he was academically gifted, he'd sped right through his degrees and then focused on biotechnology. But he knew what he had to do, what she needed right now. Unfortunately, he had very few resources or equipment to help her as much as she needed.

He turned off the water and dried them both the best he could with the threadbare towels in the bathroom, and then carried Ellie to the only bed in the house, the one that had been denied to her because of her confinement. Pulling back the bedspread, he was relieved that the bedcovers looked fairly clean, and he tucked her beneath the blanket and the sheets. Sitting beside her, he attempted to comb her long hair with his fingers. Ellie had beautiful, light-blonde hair, and he was starting to see the fair locks again now that it was clean. Pushing the hair away from her face, he was practically ready to go ballistic over the healing bruises and cuts on her skin.

He'd looked her over while he was washing her, and he hadn't seen anything life-threatening as far as injuries, but it fucking pissed him off that James had even touched Ellie.

Zane rose and went to work cleaning up the mess in the corner, washing down the floor and disposing of the metal bindings and the portable potty. When he was done, he wrapped a blanket around his nude body, put on his boots, and sprinted back out to his SUV, grabbing the overnight bag that he always had in the cargo space.

He dressed in the spare clothing he had, wishing he had something more he could put on Ellie except one of his flannel shirts that was tucked away inside the bag.

After he got her into the garment, he gave her a little more fluid, and then went and rummaged through the small dwelling, trying to find anything useful. He came across Ellie's purse in one of the cupboards, but he didn't see any sign of her clothing. Zane put his dirty garments in the sink and washed them by hand, and then hung them in the bathroom to dry. He didn't think he'd need them because he planned on getting Ellie down the mountain soon. It was more his restless energy that wouldn't let him keep still.

He found some basic supplies, mostly canned goods, but at least there was something.

Since the antiquated heating system was producing very little warmth, he loaded the old stove with wood that was stacked against the wall and started a fire that was soon blazing. He shut the metal door, glad that the old piece of crap actually worked. The cabin was so small that it should help keep the limited space warmer.

Having rummaged through every cupboard, Zane paced back and forth from the bedroom to the small window beside the door, wishing it would fucking stop snowing.

Ellie needs so much more than I can do for her right now. She needs IV fluids and feedings, x-rays, and testing.

Hell, he knew she was bad, but he had no idea if her body had more wrong than what he could see just from looking at her and doing a superficial exam.

Unfortunately, the blizzard was still raging, and he was frustrated that there was little he could do except keep giving Ellie everything he could in intervals that wouldn't overfill her shrunken stomach.

He helped her swallow some nourishment.

Then he paced.

He did it again.

Then he paced.

He kept trying his cell phone, but he was in a dead zone, and he didn't want to leave Ellie to try to attempt to find an area that could pick up a signal. More than likely, nothing would be close. He was pretty sure this whole desolate mountain area was off the grid.

As it started getting dark, he fired up an ancient generator that would give them some light, and then fed the hungry stove more wood, noticing that the tiny dwelling was already getting warmer.

As he sat back down on the bed to heft Ellie up to drink some more, he was elated to see that she was swallowing more readily.

"Come on, Ellie. Just a little more," he crooned, trying to cajole her into a few more swallows.

She complied, and he set the cup on a small, rustic bedside table.

"Zane?" The weak voice was barely a whisper.

But he heard it.

His head jerked toward Ellie, his heart racing as he saw her eyelids flicker before she opened them completely.

A look of horror crossed her face for just a moment until she focused in on him. "Zane?" she asked again uncertainly, her whisper panicked and scared.

"Yeah. It's me, Ellie. It's Zane." He stroked a gentle hand over her hair. "You're safe. Don't be afraid." *Jesus!* He hated seeing that terrified look on her face.

"James," she rasped.

He put his fingers over her lips. "Don't try to talk. James is dead. He can never hurt you again. You have to rest, Ellie. I've been trying to rehydrate you. You're pretty weak, and I need to get you to the hospital. The weather is shit. Just rest until I can get you out of here, okay?"

She nodded feebly, as though she understood him, and her eyes fluttered closed.

Zane went to rise from the bed, but Ellie said softly, "Don't go, Zane. Please. I think I'm hallucinating, but I want it to last."

Kicking off his boots, he pivoted and stretched his body out next to hers. "You're not dreaming, and me being here is no illusion. James is dead and he's never coming back. I can't take you down the mountain right now. We're in a blizzard. But I'll get you to safety as fast as I can."

He gently wrapped his arms around her and placed her head on his chest, smoothing his hand rhythmically over her now-dry hair.

"I think I'm already safe," she said hesitantly, snuggling into his body.

"Damn right you are. I won't let anything happen to you, Ellie. I promise."

She sighed lightly, and then her breathing became even and deep. Zane knew that she was sleeping, no longer in an unconscious state.

Relief flowed over him as his body relaxed. He put both arms protectively around Ellie, rocking her body gently in an effort to comfort her, but maybe just a little bit for himself, too, because he was so damn grateful that she was alive.

Finally, with Ellie cuddled safe and warm against him, Zane slept.

Chapter 2

E llie opened her eyes, confused.

Where am I? What happened?

James!

Panic seized her as she looked around, terrified that it was James's return to the cabin that had woken her. Fear and dread seized her by the throat, but she noticed her mouth was no longer as dry as the desert.

Pulse racing, her breathing erratic, Ellie's reaction was pure terror. Frantically, she started to look around the cabin, hoping there was nobody here.

Except…she wasn't in the cabin anymore. Her rational mind started to function and she slowly tried to take in her surroundings.

It didn't take her long to realize she was in the hospital, medical personnel scurrying around and passing the open door to the hallway at a pace that made her dizzy.

The white sheets and blankets that were covering her helped verify her location, as did the IV in her arm and all of the wires attached to her body.

She started to feel terror welling up inside her, not understanding why she was here or how she got to a hospital, when she heard *his* voice.

"Thank fuck! You're awake."

Her head jerked up to see an exhausted-looking Zane Colter at her bedside, his clothing rumbled and his hair mussed, as though he'd been running his hand through it over and over again.

Her suspicion was confirmed when he raked his hand through his hair again, either in relief or frustration. Sometimes with Zane, it was hard to tell what he was thinking. But stoic or not, she was glad he was here, and she felt her body relax for the first time in a very long time.

"What happened?" Her voice was as weak as her body. "How did I get here?"

"You don't remember anything?" Zane asked with a frown.

Ellie probed her brain, vaguely remembering hearing Zane's voice telling her everything would be okay. "I thought you were a dream."

"I hardly think I'm anybody's dream," Zane said drily.

Ellie suddenly remembered how she had gotten in her current condition in the first place, horrifying memories flowing back into her brain as she struggled to sit up in bed. "Oh, God. I have to talk to Chloe. James—"

He pushed her back down gently. She didn't have the strength to really move, much less sit up.

"Is dead," Zane finished. "He killed himself, Ellie. Before that, he was in the hospital because he was stupid enough to hurt our sister. That's why you didn't get food and water. You were in bad shape when I finally found you in that cabin."

"Chloe—"

"My little sister is on her honeymoon. She married Gabe Walker, a man who will take good care of her."

Ellie's head was spinning by the time he caught her up on what had happened to Chloe, and how she'd been blackmailed. She'd missed so much, and so many things had happened while she'd been held captive by James.

"Thank God," Ellie whispered and let her head fall back onto the pillow. "After I saw those videos, I was so afraid for her."

"He knew that you knew about them?"

Ellie nodded. "He caught me with his laptop. I was on my way to Chloe when he kidnapped me at the office and tossed me in the trunk of his vehicle."

"Christ!" Zane cursed vehemently.

"I was unconscious for a while, so I didn't know how far he'd driven. I didn't even know exactly where he had me hidden. All I knew was that I was in some sort of cabin, and I assumed it was remote. I never did figure out why he didn't just kill me."

"Insurance," Zane grumbled. "I have no doubt that after the wedding, he would have stopped caring whether you were alive or dead."

"Everybody thought I was dead?" she asked quietly.

"Pretty much," he agreed. "But Chloe and I never stopped looking. Since your car was missing, most people assumed you had either left or were already dead."

Ellie shuddered. Her poor *Blue Turtle* had been in the office parking lot. Obviously, James had gotten rid of it. "I think I *was* almost dead. Toward the end, I wasn't sure whether I wanted James to come back, or just let me die." His visits hadn't been frequent, but they'd always been painful.

"Don't say that," Zane rasped. "I know he beat the crap out of you. Did he rape you, Ellie?"

"No," she told him, embarrassed. "I was too fat for him in the beginning, and I think he got more joy out of torturing me. Once I got thinner, he told me I was a dirty, disgusting pig."

Zane stroked her hair absently. "I'm so damn sorry I didn't find you earlier."

She smiled up at him weakly. "I'm grateful you found me *at all.*" She hesitated before saying, "I wonder what he did with my car. He could have taken my keys, but I wonder where he hid my old *Blue Turtle.*"

"Your what?" Zane answered, confused.

Ellie sighed. "I called my car my *Blue Turtle.* I had it for so long, but it just kept on going. It just got a little slower over time."

"It was never found," Zane confirmed.

"I assume that once you found me, you brought me here. Where are we?"

"Denver. It was closer, and has medical facilities better equipped for the condition you were in. I did what I could the first night of the blizzard, but when you still weren't coherent the next day, I headed down from the mountain. The snow had let up some, and I had to take the chance of getting you somewhere for treatment."

"I lost track of time. How long did James keep me there?" Ellie had lost her senses a little at a time, and the days and nights had all run together.

"About seven months," Zane answered reluctantly.

Ellie's mouth dropped open in shock. For a while, she'd counted the days and weeks that passed, but eventually she'd slept most of the time when James wasn't there. After she'd tried everything she could think of to get herself free, her hopes of being rescued had faded. Little by little, her energy had gotten depleted, and she'd started rationing her food and water, never knowing when she'd get some again…or if she *ever* would.

"My mom. She's probably been heartsick." If she'd been missing for months, her poor mother was probably worried.

"I called her. Saying she was happy would be an understatement. She's on her way here from Montana." He waited a moment before he asked, "Do you want me to tell Chloe?"

"No," she answered immediately. "She deserves her time away after what happened with James. It sounds like she's healing. I can see her when she gets back. I hope I'm healthier when I finally see her."

Ellie didn't need a mirror to know she looked hideous, and the last thing she wanted was for Chloe to blame herself. Now that she knew the whole story, Ellie knew Chloe had been through enough. Although Ellie desperately wanted her best friend, she didn't want her to see her this way. Knowing Chloe, she'd blame herself.

"We haven't told them anything. She doesn't even know James is dead. I have a feeling Blake probably told Gabe." Zane sounded slightly uncomfortable. "But I think she might be pissed that I didn't tell her that I found you."

"It's probably better that way, even if she's a little angry. I'll tell her it was my idea. Once she feels more together, she'll be able to handle everything better. She might not fuss as much if I'm stronger."

"I think she might feel better knowing you're alive," Zane answered drily.

"Not yet. Please." Ellie knew Chloe, and she'd be heartsick if she saw her right now, emaciated and torn up from James's frequent beatings. She didn't want her best friend to see her as she was now, not when Chloe had been through so much herself.

"Stop worrying about Chloe. She's doing a hell of a lot better than you are right now. Do *you* need anything?" Zane asked hesitantly, looking impatient, like he needed something to occupy himself.

She was going to need a lot of things, but she refused to think about that right now. "No. How long have I been here?"

"Two days," he answered gruffly.

"I don't remember," she admitted, unable to recall her transport to the hospital.

"Totally understandable," Zane informed her. "You were confused because of the dehydration. Luckily, there shouldn't be any permanent damage once you're completely healed. Now that you're getting what you need, everything will correct itself. It will take time to put some weight back on, and you'll need time to recover from the weakness, but it's all reversible."

Ellie noticed that Zane looked completely done in. His expression was weary, his eyes were bloodshot, and there were shadows beneath those expressive gray eyes.

"Have you slept at all? You have a house here in Denver, right? Maybe you should go home and get some rest." Even as she said the words, her heart lurched at the thought of him leaving her alone. Rationally, she knew she was out of danger, but she selfishly wanted Zane to stay with her for a little while longer.

"Do you honestly think I'm going anywhere? Jesus! I tore up most of Colorado looking for you. I'm not leaving," he said stubbornly, crossing his arms over his broad chest.

"Then at least sleep tonight." She glanced out the window, noticing it was dark. There was an extra bed in the room right next to her.

"I can't believe you're worried about me. Christ, Ellie. You nearly died, and spent seven months in chains. Me getting some sleep is not a fucking priority."

She knew if she started to relive the last several months, she'd end up a mess. "Sometimes it's easier not to think about it. I'm here now. I'm alive. All because of you. I'm getting good care, and I'm awake and talking. There's no reason for you not to rest."

"I'll lie down once you sleep again. I have a feeling it won't be long."

Ellie's eyelids were already feeling heavy, but she fought the welcoming void of darkness, where she knew she'd forget what happened for the moment. "When can I go home?"

"When the doctors say it's safe," Zane said testily.

"I don't even know if I still *have* a home. I have no vehicle. I don't have a job." She started to hyperventilate as she thought about all she'd lost. She had been broke before she took the job with James, and she hadn't worked there long enough to even get her first check.

"Don't worry about any of that right now," Zane ordered firmly. "Everything will work itself out. You can come home with me. You won't have fully regained your strength when you leave here, and you still have injuries to heal and nutritional deficiencies."

Her chin lifted. "I can take care of myself." The last thing Ellie needed was Zane's pity.

"You're going to be stubborn after everything that's happened? You can't take a little help from friends?"

"I may not have a choice," Ellie admitted. She didn't know if her apartment was still hers, she had no source of income, and no way to even get around to apply for a job.

"As far as I'm concerned, you don't have options. I'm taking you home with me even if I have to toss you over my shoulder and drag you there. You need help, and after what happened, I don't want you out of my sight."

Friends? Were she and Zane really friends? Yeah, back in high school she would have said they were, even though she'd also been majorly infatuated with him. But she'd only seen him a handful of times since then, and they hadn't spoken much. Really, he was the brother of her best friend and just some guy she'd had a crush on in her early years of high school. He had no reason to be stuck to her like glue. Nevertheless, he obviously cared about what happened to her.

"I'm glad you're here," Ellie confessed. "I'm feeling a little lost." Actually she was feeling *plenty* lost, but didn't want to admit it. Since she was physically weak, the obstacles in front of her seemed overwhelming. Psychologically, she was finding herself almost incapable of not panicking about her future.

"Someday, you'll have to deal with what happened to you. But that day is *not* today. You need rest and you need to get well. I'll be right here. I'm not going anywhere," Zane told her tenaciously.

Ellie shuddered, dreading the time when she'd need to deal with her confinement, the memories of never knowing if the next time James came to the cabin he'd bring supplies…or just kill her off.

Feeling like she had heavy weights on her eyelids, she gave up the struggle of staying awake and closed them. "Someday," she whispered, wondering if she'd ever be strong enough to actually talk about her experiences when trying to forget seemed so much easier.

"Sleep, Ellie," Zane said in a deep, hypnotic voice, his hand reaching for hers. He clasped it tightly.

Her first instinct was to flinch away from his touch since every bit of human contact in the last seven months had led to pain. Eventually, the gentleness of his comforting gesture made her relax again. She tried to squeeze his fingers, but everything was too much effort. Taking comfort in the fact that Zane was nearby, she slept.

Ellie spent a lot of time sleeping the next few days. Her mom came to see her, and they had a very joyful but short reunion since her mother had a business to help run with her husband back in Montana.

Knowing her sole parent had experienced more than her fair share of poverty in the past, the last thing Ellie wanted was for her ordeal to force her mom back into financial difficulties. Her mother still lived from day-to-day financially, never knowing how much the business was going to make that month. But Ellie was glad her mom had a warm home to sleep in, food on the table, and a husband who loved her. Her mom was finally happy, and Ellie didn't want to do anything to take away that contentment.

Aileen, the Colter matriarch, was a frequent visitor, as were Tate and Lara Colter, Chloe's youngest brother and his wife.

Chloe's sister-in-law was in the process of setting up counseling sessions for Ellie with the same therapist that she'd recommended to Chloe, a Dr. Natalie Townson. Apparently, she was one of the best psychologists in the world for women with domestic abuse issues.

Ellie wasn't sure how *domestic* her experience had been, but it had definitely been traumatic and violent. Even now, she could still see James's evil face, hear his harsh, brutal words pushing their way into her head, and remember his powerful blows. It was hard to close her eyes without seeing him, remembering everything. Little by little, her time as a captive was all coming back to her. The images were vivid at times, so real that she struggled to convince herself she was safe.

Sometimes she wished the memories had stayed hidden or vague within her brain, but whether she liked it or not, she *was* remembering. Recently, her nightmares were so intense that she woke up terrified and gasping for breath. Luckily, she'd never made much noise during her bad dreams because Zane never woke up, though he slept in the other bed in her room every single night.

Some nights, she wanted to reach out to him, but stopped herself. She'd always taken care of herself. Maybe money was tight, but she'd managed, both emotionally and physically. It was important that she get back to where she was before: a self-sufficient woman who did just fine being alone. That meant she had to learn to deal with her own issues, even the nightmares.

During the busy days of visitors and treatments at the hospital, Ellie ate just like a woman who had been deprived of food for months. Starting off slow, she'd finally progressed to solid food, and she was constantly starving. Unfortunately, the hospital food left much to be desired, but she ate every single bite, her remembered fear of going hungry and thirsty still haunting her.

Zane's constant presence was the only thing that made her feel safe. He was always around, always present. He slept in the bed next to her, his protective company easing some of the fear she felt when she woke up abruptly and was terrified. Just seeing him in a bed beside her was enough to calm herself down.

I can't cling to him. I can't get used to him being around.

She sighed as she turned off her Kindle, a gift from Zane to keep her from going stir-crazy, and set it beside the bed. Today had been quiet. Her mom had gone back to Montana, and no one had come to visit yet. Even Zane was strangely absent.

I can't expect him to sit around here and baby me forever. He's an important man with a very large company to run.

Just as the thought ran through her head, Zane came through the door, closing it behind him.

"What's that?" She nodded to the enormous bag in his arms.

"Contraband," he answered with a rare grin. "We both know hospital food sucks."

Her breath hitched as she watched a mischievous look cross his irresistibly handsome face. When Zane smiled, it was nearly infectious. At least it was for her. He was always so serious that his naughty expression made her heart skitter and warmth spread through her entire body.

Ellie watched as he pulled out several large containers of Chinese food, then some junk food, and finally a bag of her favorite specialty chocolate. He pulled paper plates from the bag and loaded one up before he placed it in front of her with plastic utensils. "Eat," he insisted as he dropped the candies next to her plate, and then pulled out a soda and opened it for her.

The smell of the Oriental cuisine made her mouth water. Chinese was her favorite. "How did you know?" He'd ordered her favorite dishes.

He hesitated before answering. "You and Chloe used to go for Chinese a lot. I figured you liked it."

"And the candy?" It was her favorite, and she didn't buy it often because it was pricey.

He shrugged. "It's chocolate, right? You like chocolate. Or at least you did when we were younger."

Ellie was convinced that it was his scientific mind that had led to a couple of very good educated guesses.

"That's my favorite, too. Thank you." Unable to wait any longer for her first decent meal in months, Ellie picked up her fork and prepared to dig into her food. "At least I won't have to feel guilty about eating a ton of carbs and chocolate."

Zane frowned at her. "Why would you feel that way at all?"

She rolled her eyes. "I used to be fat, Zane. If I keep eating like this, I'll gain all that weight back."

"Good. You were never fat. Eat," he insisted.

She *had* been overweight, but she wasn't right now, and she actually needed to put on some pounds, a novel experience for her since she had been chubby since she was a child. Being able to eat without guilt was the only bright spot in this otherwise nightmarish experience.

As she shoveled food into her mouth, she could feel Zane watching her, but when she looked at him, he looked away and started filling a plate for himself.

Between bites, she told him, "God, this is either really amazing food, or I'm so hungry that anything more edible than hospital food tastes good."

"It's good," Zane confirmed, seating himself in a chair next to her bed and starting to eat. "It's the best Asian food in the area. I've tried every one of them. It's one of my favorites, too."

Ellie watched him covertly as she ate, her heart flip-flopping just as it always did whenever she saw Zane. Now that he was her rescuer, it made her youthful infatuation spring to life again.

It's hero worship. It has to be. Zane was responsible for saving my life. I absolutely am not really attracted to him.

Irritatingly, Ellie had to acknowledge that she wasn't totally convinced her desire to devour *him* along with her food wasn't all about the fact that Zane saved her.

Something about Zane Colter had always attracted her like a giant magnet. She'd never figured out whether it was because he was amazingly smart, or if it was the fact that he was the hottest guy she'd ever seen. His dark hair was a little too long, and occasionally some of those black tresses fell onto his forehead, making him seem more approachable. He had the trademark Colter eyes, gray and ever-changing in shade, depending on his mood.

She could say Zane was nice, but one would never know it. *She* knew because she was acquainted with him, but he was often distracted or quiet, not because he was a jerk, but because he simply had nothing to say.

Ellie was pretty sure he didn't give a damn about status, or what kind of clothing he wore. Mostly, she'd seen him in jeans and flannel shirts. In the summer, he opted for a T-shirt. His big feet were usually in a pair of hiking boots, and his hair had no semblance of order or even a definitive cut. *Nope.* He definitely wasn't a guy who spent a lot of time *trying* to look trendy. He never had been. Maybe that's why she'd always liked him. He was naturally hotter than hell, but never acted like he knew it.

He had been as socially awkward as she had back in high school. While people said he was shy, she'd never seen him that way. Problem was, Zane was too smart to be happy having a conversation he thought was irrelevant. He'd been too busy trying to figure out every scientific mystery that existed on the planet. Most other high school guys had just wanted to get laid.

"I'm stuffed," she groaned as she pushed her plate back.

He looked up from his plate. "You hardly ate anything."

"My stomach is smaller," she informed him.

"You're too skinny," he replied gruffly.

Ellie laughed. "I've never had that problem before." She was still thin, but now that she was being pumped full of nutrition and hydrated, it probably wouldn't take long for her to gain weight. It never did.

She smiled at him, liking the fact that he was blunt and always said whatever he was thinking. His words were rarely censored, and he didn't seem to care whether they were tactful or not.

"They're going to let you go home in a few days. I thought we could go to my house in Denver, but it's a media circus outside. I think you'd be safer in Rocky Springs. My property there is secure, and if they set one foot on Colter land, they'll be arrested. We can take off from the helipad on the roof."

"Zane, I can't go home with you. I'll stay with Aileen for a while if I need to, try to figure out what I'm going to do. You've already lost enough time trying to find me and then taking care of me. I'm going to have to get my shit together pretty fast."

"You're staying with me, even if I have to toss you over my shoulder and take you to my house. Mom's home isn't secure. Hell, she doesn't even have an alarm system. My property is fenced. I have a small lab there, and it needed to be secure." He took her plate and started to finish off her food after dumping his own empty dish into the garbage.

"My apartment—"

"It's been rented. All of your stuff was sent to my house, and the furniture was put in storage."

Ellie's heart sank. "I didn't think my landlady would evict me."

In a kinder voice, Zane answered, "Nobody believed you were even alive anymore, Ellie. You were gone seven months. She didn't exactly evict you."

You believed it, or you wouldn't have kept searching. Ellie still wondered why Zane had kept searching when even the police had given up hope of finding her alive.

She sighed and started plucking at the white blanket nervously. "I suppose. Life moved on without me."

"Not for everybody. And never for me," Zane told her in a graveled voice as he dumped her now-empty plate and opened the bag of candy.

"Why didn't you and Chloe give up? Why didn't you just assume I was dead or gone?" Ellie knew Zane was analytical and realistic. He was a scientist. After seven months gone, the likelihood of him finding her alive had been pretty much nil. A brain that was as rational as Zane's should have told him to quit looking.

He pinned her with his intense stare, his eyes smoky and dark. He took one of the chocolates he'd unwrapped and held it to her mouth.

It was a strange sensation, having a guy feed her, but she opened her lips and sucked in the round chocolate, the explosive taste of sweetness making her bite back a moan of pleasure.

Finally, Zane answered, "Because I didn't want to believe it, Ell. Until I had positive proof that you were gone, I wasn't going to stop looking for you. It's as simple as that."

The use of his shortened version of her name surprised her. Nobody had ever called her that but him, and not since they were teenagers. She'd always kind of liked it when they were young. Ellie looked up at him, mesmerized by the fierce expression on his face. Zane was a scientist. Of course he would have wanted to find her body for her family and Chloe, but she sensed his reasons were somehow…different. Like a personal mission he wasn't willing to stop. "But there was no hope."

"Bullshit. I always had hope, Ellie. I know you well enough to know you're a fighter, and so does Chloe. Neither one of us ever believed the bullshit assumption that you just left in your vehicle and never came back. It made no sense. Both of us discounted that theory as soon as the police threw it out."

Thank God for that! If he hadn't been so tenacious, she'd be dead by now.

"Thank you," she whispered. "I'm grateful you never gave up on finding me." If he had stopped looking for her, she wouldn't have lasted much longer alone. Her doctors had told her bluntly she probably couldn't have survived another day without water, food, or warmth.

"I would have never given up," he grumbled.

He fed her another chocolate, preventing her from responding. Eventually, they needed to talk about his plans to take her home with him. Until then, she'd savor both the sweet treat and the man who had given it to her.

His desire to help her, and his gruff tenderness, were a side of Zane she'd never seen before. Of course, she'd seen little of him since he'd left for college, and he'd turned into one hell of a grown man. She'd just never spent enough time with him to realize just how special he'd grown up to be.

However, he'd done enough for her, and he'd eventually see the sense in her staying with Aileen until she was fully recovered. The media would find another story and stop hounding her after a while.

She knew she'd have to stop depending on Zane. He'd been her rescuer, and that was enough. Somehow, she'd pick herself up and recover from the damage that had been done to her body, mind, and soul.

As he offered her another piece of candy, she shook her head. She was going to have to learn to resist temptation. Somehow, she was pretty certain that avoiding chocolate wouldn't be her most difficult test in the near future, but it was definitely a place to start.

Chapter 3

Two days later, Ellie still hadn't convinced Zane to be more reasonable or sensible. Exactly when he had become so hard-headed and bossy she wasn't certain, but he could be relentless and uncompromising when he really wanted something, or thought it was the best solution.

She knew she had to either cut her ties to him now, or she'd end up needing to see him every time she was afraid.

"I'm not going home with you," Ellie told him stubbornly as a nurse pushed her toward the elevator in a wheelchair after she was discharged.

"I'm afraid you don't have much of a choice. I'm your ride out of here. The media is still camped outside the hospital. I guess you'll have to stay," Zane answered matter-of-factly as he walked beside her wheelchair.

Ellie crossed her arms and glared up at him. "You set this all up. Aileen hasn't answered her phone, and I haven't seen Tate and Lara in two days."

Zane shrugged a little, too innocently. "Maybe they're busy."

Ellie liked Zane, but he was being unreasonable and somewhat manipulative, too. "I used to like you," she mumbled under her breath.

"Did you say something?" he inquired politely.

"No. Look, you know I want to go back to Rocky Springs. You're probably needed *here* in your lab. It makes no sense for me to stay at your place alone. I don't even have a car anymore, and I need to be able to get around. I have to look for a job, straighten out everything that was left undone. This isn't even reasonable. You've done enough for me, Zane."

"Until you're better, I'll be there, Ellie," Zane rasped as they exited up a ramp and onto the rooftop. He plucked her out of the wheelchair, nodded to the nurse, a woman who had been completely silent and disappeared just as quietly.

Ellie was confused as Zane deposited her into a sleek helicopter, dropped her bag with what few belongings she had with her in the backseat, and then hopped into the pilot's position.

"We're really flying home?" she squeaked, still stunned as he put on a pair of headphones with a microphone attached, and carefully placed another on her head.

"It's a long drive. I'm not going to make you go through the media mob and then have you sit in a vehicle that long." He methodically buckled her in, and then secured his own straps. "I told you we'd fly out."

She startled as she heard his low, husky voice through the headphones. Zane *had* told her that he'd fly her from a helicopter off the roof, but the reality of that scenario had never registered with Ellie. Because Chloe had been her friend most of their lives, it was easy to forget just how ridiculously wealthy the Colter family really was. For being ultra-rich, most of the family was down-to-earth. Sure, they owned a large amount of property, but none of them acted like wealthy snobs. Chloe was the sweetest woman Ellie had ever known, and she hated the lives of the super-rich. Her friend would rather be with her beloved horses than at a party with other rich people.

As the aircraft started up, she asked him curiously, "Can you really pilot this thing?" *Didn't most rich guys have a pilot?*

He shrugged. "Of course. It makes it more efficient to get around. I have a pilot for my jet, but I generally fly myself in the helicopter and small planes. I might not be the hotshot pilot that Tate is, but I'm competent enough." He started doing checks, and communicating with what she assumed was some kind of air traffic control center.

Ellie had no doubt Zane was skilled at everything he did. When they finally lifted off, her stomach felt like it had dropped to her feet. "Oh, God. I've never flown before." She put a hand to her belly.

"Are you going to be okay?" His voice sounded concerned.

When they leveled off, Ellie's fear started to drift away as she looked down at the scenery below after they left the Denver metro area. "Yeah. I mean, I'm not going to get sick or anything. This is just…different."

"Hang in there. It's not that long by helicopter."

"Take your time," she said breathlessly, overwhelmed by the experience of viewing Colorado from so high up. "It's kind of amazing."

"You've really never flown before? Not even in a commercial plane?"

"No. I've never been out of Colorado." Honestly, she'd never gone far from her hometown. "When things got really bad and I was sure I was going to die, one of my regrets was that I never got to see much outside of Rocky Springs."

"What other regrets did you have?" he asked hoarsely.

That I never got to kiss you!

Ellie wasn't about to reveal all of the epiphanies she'd had when she thought her time on Earth was done. "Lots of things. It's strange what you think about when you suddenly realize how little you've done in your life, and you're pretty sure you're going to die."

"What?" he persisted.

Ellie sighed. "I was just starting a small side business when James abducted me. It wasn't doing a lot, but it was slowly growing. I was sorry I hadn't started it earlier so I could see how people liked my products." She paused before adding, "And I've never really been in love, or had a guy who was crazy enough about me to actually romance me." She'd never gotten flowers or even a romantic dinner. "And I've never been kissed so passionately that I could forget the rest of the world and come out of it breathless," she admitted reluctantly.

"You've dated," Zane argued.

"Some," she conceded. "But it was all pretty casual. I was overweight, so I wasn't exactly attractive enough to turn many heads, and the guys who wanted to go out with me got bored pretty quickly. I don't exactly lead an exciting life, and I was usually more interested in working on my new business than going out."

"You've always been beautiful, Ell. What kind of business?"

There was that intimate nickname again, and his casual comment about how she looked surprised her.

"Just a little online thing. I make candles, essential oils, lotions, and soaps. I dabble a little with personal fragrances, but most of it revolves around aromatherapy." She looked out the window, noticing that they were getting into areas with sparser populations, and she was awed by the view of the snow-covered peaks of the front range of the Rocky Mountains. Even though she saw them all the time, they looked different from the air.

"You believe in the healing powers of scents?"

Ellie couldn't tell if Zane was laughing at her or just curious. "To a point," she answered honestly. "I don't think it's actually a cure for diseases, but I think certain scents can affect moods and create a sense of well-being. It's something I've been interested in for years, and everything I know is from self-study. But I love making the products. I love making people feel…happier."

"You did all that from that tiny apartment?" Zane started to descend once he reached the valleys in between the peaks.

"Yeah. It wasn't easy. I'm pretty sure all of my supplies and equipment are gone now."

"They will be at my house," he assured her. "Nothing got thrown away."

"I'm sure I got hammered in emails by a few customers since there were some orders that I didn't deliver since I was…" She swallowed hard. "Unavailable."

Zane expertly maneuvered the aircraft onto the small airstrip and set them gently down on the ground.

"Everything will be okay," he said confidently. "Give it time, Ellie."

She pulled off her headphones, wondering how Zane always seemed to know what she was thinking. Her insecurity must be showing, because she still felt lost. And for some odd reason, Zane seemed to sense it.

Someone must have dropped off his vehicle, because he shifted her directly from the seat of the helicopter into a black SUV.

Reflexively, she briefly flinched as he swept her into his strong arms, a knee-jerk reaction that she hadn't been able to completely lose when anybody touched her. Her heart lurched as she relaxed and put her arms around his neck, her face so close to him that she could get drunk on his masculine scent. "I am capable of walking, you know," she told him nervously. The feel of his powerful body cradling her in his arms felt way too good, way too safe.

He scowled down at her. "In those flimsy shoes? Not happening."

What she was wearing was little more than slippers, but there was no snow on the runway.

She didn't argue as he put her in the passenger seat of his SUV as some guy she didn't know came jogging out of a hangar to take care of the helicopter. Most likely, he was an employee. Since she had spent zero time at the airfield on Colter land, she wasn't sure.

Zane's vehicle was running and warm, and Ellie was starting to get overheated from the layers of clothing Zane had insisted she wear because it was a cold day. She pulled the hat off her head and unwrapped the scarf around her neck, placing both items in her lap before unzipping her down jacket. They were all items Zane had brought with him to take her home.

Zane slid into the driver's seat and quickly closed the door. "We'll be home shortly. Are you okay?"

"Fine," she reassured him. "But I don't really have a home anymore."

"You have mine," Zane growled as he put the vehicle in motion. "You don't have to be so damn stubborn. It's the safest place for you to be right now."

"I'm not trying to be stubborn or morose. It's just really disorienting to know I really have nowhere to go that's actually mine anymore. Can't you understand that?"

"Yes. It's understandable. But it's one thing you really don't need to consider right now. You'll get better, and then you can take on the world."

Ellie sat back in the seat, knowing she was going to have to accept her temporary home with Zane. Obviously his family was in agreement with his plan, and had cooperated so he could get what he wanted. Although she was angry because Zane was so highhanded, she was still grateful that he cared enough to open his home to her. How many busy, rich guys would make the time for her that Zane had? *Why* he was taking so much time and effort for her she still didn't understand, but she couldn't just discard his kindness. "Thank you."

"It's no trouble. I have to be here for the rest of the holidays, and I have a small lab here where I can work."

"You work here, too?"

"Yeah. Mostly personal projects, things that are going to take ongoing study and replication."

"Like what?" she asked curiously. "Do you like what you're doing? I know you were obsessed with changing the world with science when we were younger. Are you still?"

Zane shrugged. "Pretty much. But I was pretty naïve, even when I was in college. I didn't realize how much crap can go along with science."

"What?" Scientific study had always been Zane's life. Ellie had never heard him talk about the downside.

"Irresponsible studies. Bullshit reports. Some places putting out supposed scientific studies without enough evidence and no replication. No real control groups and not big enough groups to even be accurate. So many scientific studies are badly conducted just for sensationalism or monetary gain. Just because a single test on mice or rats shows something that's a possibility doesn't mean it's always true for humans, but the media will blow it up until everything is skewed to be taken as the truth."

"But businesses want to be profitable, I suppose," Ellie mused, touched by how seriously Zane took his profession.

"My lab is very profitable, but it can be profitable and ethical at the same time," Zane said adamantly.

"So my being at your home won't really make you wish you could be at your main lab because you have one set up at home?"

"Even if I didn't, my priority is to see you recover. Nobody deserves what happened to you. And you were completely faultless. Wrong place at the wrong damn time."

"Why are you doing all of this? I don't understand," she finally asked. "It's not like we've seen much of each other since you graduated from high school. We really aren't friends."

"Because I want to," he answered enigmatically.

"Why?" She leaned her head back against the headrest, feeling both emotionally and physically tired.

"*You* may not consider *me* your friend, but I've never stopped thinking of *you* as *mine*. You've helped me in the past. You never treated me differently in high school even though I was a weird science nerd. You helped me organize some of my high school research projects, and you were always nice to me. I never stopped being your friend just because I moved away," he said huskily.

Ellie's heart melted as she sensed the insecurity in his words. Zane had been a loner when he was a teen, mostly because he was more interested in science than people. But not many of the kids at school had really gotten to know him. Deep inside, Zane had been a kind, quirky, intelligent adolescent, and as he matured, he obviously hadn't changed. Granted, he'd become a lot bossier and determined to have his way. But the heart of the young man she'd known hadn't really altered.

"I never stopped thinking of you as a friend, either," she admitted, knowing she had thought about him a lot more than she should have over the years. "You were always nice to me, too, even though I was overweight and not very popular in high school. It meant a lot to me."

Actually, all of Chloe's brothers had been nice. But since Marcus and Blake were older, they'd been graduating when she and Chloe were just starting high school. Tate had always been sweet, but the girls had always been drawn to him, and he'd practically had his own harem, even in high school. Since Chloe, Tate, and Zane were so close in age, Ellie had always wondered how Chloe's mom could have survived being constantly pregnant for well over two years.

Tate was younger, closer in age to her and Chloe, but she'd never had more than a casual acquaintance with him. It was Zane who had caught her attention back then, probably because he was so much more approachable, so much more like her. He was almost always alone, and probably felt like he didn't fit in. They'd struck up a friendship when she'd seen his frustration at the tediousness of organizing his research. She'd offered to help put everything in a likely order after questioning him about the different portions of his notes. Even though the material was way over her head, she had put things in a logical order, which didn't take a genius.

He shrugged. "I liked you. And I don't like all that many people."

Ellie laughed at his bluntness, a part of Zane she secretly adored. He wasn't much for small talk. If he appeared socially awkward sometimes, she attributed that to his intelligence. He didn't communicate on the same level as most people did. It wasn't that he couldn't; he just didn't, probably because most people were too intimidated to have a conversation with him. If she didn't know him, Ellie wondered how daunting it might be to approach a man who had one of the smartest scientific brains in the country. Fortunately, she knew there was so much more to him than just the geeky science nerd he claimed to be.

As Ellie thought about all of the things Chloe had shared with her about her brothers over the years, she suddenly remembered something, a fact that had eluded her until today. "Don't you have a girlfriend who'll be upset if I'm staying with you? Isn't she coming here for the holidays?" she asked curiously.

"No. I'm not interested in a woman who just pretends to like me for my money or Colter status."

Her heart sank as she thought about the fact that women probably *did* pursue him just because he was a billionaire Colter. "Not all women are like that, Zane. Haven't you met somebody you just connected with on another level?"

"No," he said simply.

"But you've dated. Chloe told me you had a girlfriend at one time." Ellie could still remember how she'd felt when she knew Zane was getting serious with a woman from Denver. Even though she hadn't seen him in a long time, Ellie had still felt an odd sense of…loss.

"I did. But it didn't last long. She got bored and moved on to someone else. She found out I didn't live a glamorous life full of endless parties and exotic vacations. After a while, she figured out I actually worked. A lot. I gave her all of the material things and money she wanted, but not the lifestyle she'd dreamed about."

Ellie crossed her arms angrily. "Then she wasn't worthy of you. Good riddance, I say." She hesitated before asking, "Did she hurt you?"

He was silent for a moment, as though he was considering her question. Finally, he said, "Not really. That was when I figured out I was better off without a relationship. Now I just fuck and forget about anything long-term."

He tried to sound nonchalant, but Ellie could hear the underlying sadness in his voice. The girlfriend *had* hurt him, and she'd made him cautious and wary. "I'm sorry she hurt you," Ellie said quietly.

"She didn't hurt me," he argued huskily.

"Yes, she did. But she just wasn't the right woman. I think there's someone for everybody if you're lucky enough to find them," Ellie replied wistfully.

"Then why are you still single?" he grunted.

"I was waiting. Someday I'm hoping somebody will really *see* me, and not just what I look like on the outside."

"You're fucking beautiful. If anybody sees you any differently, they're an idiot."

"I'm plain, I was chubby, and now I'm too skinny. I'm not much for going to bars or parties. I'd rather be reading a good book or making candles most of the time. Does that sound exciting to you?" she asked drily.

"There's nothing wrong with being different, Ell," Zane replied gruffly.

"I could say the same thing to you," she answered lightly, but her heart was smiling from his words.

He didn't answer as he pulled up to the entrance of his enormous home. The iron gates were incredibly high and the posts along the top looked sharp. Nobody sane was going over one of the walls of his fortress.

She watched as he punched in a code and the iron gates began to swing open.

"Paranoid much?" she asked curiously.

"I have to be. I've had people try to steal my research too many times. I can't use electric fences because of the wildlife, but it's as safe here as possible."

Ellie could believe that. She saw video cameras and motion lights click on as they went down the driveway. "Is it that bad?"

"Bad enough to be cautious," he answered as he pulled his vehicle into a massive garage. "Since I keep a research lab here, I'm careful. I'm rich enough, and my lab has made me even richer. I might not care about the money, but there's a lot of it to be had with the right research in biotech."

"Your lab here…it's in the house?" Not that she doubted that a lab *would* fit *inside* the enormous mansion she'd gotten a brief look at on the way down the drive. But it was getting late, and it got dark early in the winter. She hadn't seen much except the enormous size.

He shook his head as he shut off the engine. "Not in the main living area. It's underground."

Ellie held up a hand when he headed toward the passenger side to help her out. "I can walk. I want to." After lying in bed for so long, it felt good to be up and walking.

He frowned. "The doctor said no heavy physical exertion for a few weeks."

She gave him a stubborn look. "I hardly think that walking qualifies as heavy physical exertion. I'm fine. Really. Please."

Reluctantly, he grabbed her bag in the backseat and unlocked the door, waiting for her to walk around the SUV. He hovered as she went up the few steps in the garage and into the house.

"Shit!"

Ellie heard the low, frustrated curse behind her. "What?"

"I forgot to have somebody come over and clean things up. The house is kind of a mess," he answered sheepishly.

She stopped and turned around, tears springing to her eyes. "Do you think I care about that? You're giving me a temporary home. I'm grateful."

It was hard to believe he cared about the fact that he hadn't cleaned up because she was going to be here.

"I care. You deserve better after the shithole you were forced to endure for months." He dropped the bag on the floor of the entry hallway and advanced until her back was against the wall. "You've been through hell and back. I want you to have some of the things you didn't have while you were held prisoner by that psychotic asshole."

Ellie sighed when he was close enough to smell, and then close enough to touch. "What are you doing?" She looked up at him curiously as he put a hand on each side of the wall, temporarily surrounding her with his heat.

His expression was intense, his smoldering gray eyes hot enough to incinerate her on the spot. "Giving you something you've never had. I'm going for breathless. Kiss me, Ellie," he demanded as a few dark locks of his hair fell to the very top of his eyes.

"W-why?" she stammered, wanting nothing else except to obey his command. She wanted his hard body pressed against her, his mouth on hers, making her feel alive again.

There was no fleeting second of panic as he imprisoned her. He wasn't touching her. But dear God, she wanted him to touch her... desperately.

"Because I said so," he replied arrogantly. "I want to give you something you've never had. A lot of things, actually."

"Am I supposed to obey your every command?" she said, stalling because she couldn't believe he was looking at her like he really *wanted* to kiss her. Just staring at the ferocious expression on his face nearly made her breathless.

"No. It would be easier if you did, but I know that's never going to happen." As soon as the words left his mouth, he lowered his head, his lips so close to hers that she could feel the heat of his breath on her face.

The sensations bombarding her made her shudder. Slowly, her hands crept up his chest. She pushed his wayward hair back from his eyes, and then wrapped her arms around his neck. "You don't have to do this because it was some silly, unfulfilled wish of mine when I thought I was dying," she whispered nervously.

"I'm not. I'm doing this for me, too," he informed her brusquely before he cradled the back of her head and then lowered his mouth to hers.

Chapter 4

His embrace was everything Ellie had ever dreamed of…and so much more. Mesmerized by the heat of his mouth, she opened to him and let him explore with his tongue, the demanding sweetness of his possession almost bringing her to her knees. If he hadn't wrapped one of his arms around her waist, she might have actually swooned like an idiot.

She *did* forget everything else except the pulsating blood pumping through her veins and the feel of Zane's demanding embrace.

She wanted the kiss to last forever, but he pulled back and gently nipped at her lips before fusing their mouths again with more tenderness than Ellie had ever known.

When he finally stepped back, Ellie's entire body was trembling, and she was *definitely* breathless.

"Is your wish fulfilled?" Zane rasped, low and sensual.

"Y-yes," she stammered as she struggled to breathe normally again, her brain and body still reeling.

"You forgot everything else? You got breathless?"

"Completely," she admitted in a rush. "What about you? You said this wasn't just for me."

He nodded. "I'm satisfied…for now."

Zane picked up her bag and took her hand, leading her through the enormous kitchen and into the living room.

Neither one of them seemed to want to speak, as though it might ruin the magical connection that had just happened in the hallway. *It was amazing for me, but maybe it was just a kiss for him.*

Telling herself she was being silly to analyze a simple kiss, she said, "This house is enormous." The ceiling was vaulted so high she had to crane her neck to see it.

Zane took off his jacket and then reached out to help her remove hers. "It's big," he conceded. "I'll give you a tour."

Ellie was rendered speechless as he led her through some of the downstairs bedrooms, each one the size of her old apartment and with their own baths. The master bedroom had a door leading to a hot springs area, something every Colter seemed to have in their homes. But when they finally entered an enormous marble tiled room with an indoor pool, she gasped. "This is unbelievable." She couldn't imagine being able to swim year-round.

"There's a gym through that door." He pointed at an entrance on the far side of the room.

By the time he'd finished the tour, even showing her the room upstairs where her belongings were being kept, Ellie was exhausted. She followed him back downstairs and to the kitchen wearily.

"Do you want me to take the room with my stuff?" she asked uncertainly.

"Hell, no. It's a mess up there. You can sort it out when you feel better. Take one of the bedrooms downstairs. Then you don't have to climb up and down the stairs all the time. Do you want your clothes?"

Ellie shook her head slowly. None of her old stuff would fit anymore. "I'll go through them tomorrow." She'd salvage whatever she could.

She could feel the tension between the two of them and Ellie wondered if she should just have him show her to her room and go to bed.

"I'm not going to apologize for kissing you," Zane said quietly, rocking back on his heels as he put his hands in the front pockets of his jeans.

Ellie was startled by the abrupt change of subject, but he'd obviously been thinking as much about that kiss as she had during their tour of the house. They'd both discarded their outerwear before the tour had started, but Ellie was still overheated as she stared at Zane's stubborn expression, her eyes unable to keep from drifting down his muscular body as he finally leaned a hip against the kitchen counter and crossed his arms in front of him, stretching the material of the beautiful green sweater he was wearing.

"I didn't ask you to," she answered quickly. "And I'm not apologizing for kissing you back." She was silent for a few seconds before she ventured, "Maybe we should just try to forget that it happened. Everything has been pretty emotional since you found me."

"I'll never forget it," he told her gutturally. "Sometimes I can't stop looking at you because I still can't believe you're here, that you're really alive. I had to touch you, Ell." He paused for a heart-stopping moment, looking like he wanted to say more about his motivations, but didn't. Abruptly, he turned toward the refrigerator and changed the topic, his voice casual again. "Now let's see if there's any food in the house. I have no idea what's here."

"I'm not that hungry," Ellie protested, confused by Zane's confession. Maybe everything still felt as surreal to him as it did to her. Maybe they just momentarily needed some kind of connection.

"Doesn't matter. You need to eat." He turned around and strode back to the hallway and picked up her belongings bag from the hospital and made his way back to the hallway with the bedrooms, Ellie following behind him. He stopped in one to drop off her bag. "You can stay in here," he instructed as he stopped at the doorway on his way out of the suite. "I'm just down the hall." He pointed to the master bedroom with the hot springs.

The suite he'd given her was a beautiful, enormous room with a sitting area and its own private bathroom. Ellie didn't have much time to check it out because Zane grasped her hand and pulled her back out to the kitchen.

She watched as he rummaged through the cupboards and rifled through the fridge. She smiled because he looked so damn adorable as he scrutinized everything, looking like he wasn't sure what any of the packages were or what to do with them.

"Let me guess…you don't cook?" She crossed her arms and rested her ass against the counter.

He turned his head and gave her a questioning look. "How did you know?"

"Maybe because you just passed over plenty of edible items, but ignored every one of them because it requires some kind of preparation." She moved to the refrigerator. "Move," she insisted, bumping him out of her way with her hip.

She inspected the contents of the freezer, noticing there wasn't much in the fridge. "You don't really have anything defrosted, but I could manage breakfast for dinner." He had plenty of eggs, cheese, and some sliced ham. There were a few potatoes that looked fairly recent, too.

"I'm not picky," he agreed readily. "Show me how and I'll do it."

"You seriously can't cook?" she asked curiously. "How do you eat?"

He shrugged. "In Denver, I order out or get stuff I can toss in the microwave. I have a housekeeper who takes pity on me and leaves me meals that I can just nuke most of the time. When I'm here, I usually have stuff around for sandwiches. I guess I ran out."

Ellie pulled out a carton of eggs and some other items before searching for a large frying pan. Somehow it seemed funny that a guy with his IQ couldn't cook an egg.

He's a billionaire. He doesn't need to cook for himself.

Ellie couldn't even imagine what it was like to have so much money that someone could just hire someone to do everyday tasks. Strangely, it didn't seem like he had a housekeeper here in Rocky Springs. When he'd said the house was a mess, he was right. The place could use a good cleaning, and there were stacks of papers and various items that had never been organized everywhere.

He watched as she worked, hovering as though she might fall over at any moment. It was as endearing as it was irritating.

"I'm fine, Zane. Really. I feel better just being able to be out of bed and on my feet." Finding a task to do for him made her feel less tired and useless, and it took her mind off her troubles.

"I never thought about getting the house ready, or having somebody leave us dinner," he grumbled.

"It doesn't matter," she answered honestly. "I want to help out while I'm here."

"You're supposed to be resting."

"Cooking a simple meal isn't hard labor," she told him jokingly. "Sit." She motioned toward the kitchen table.

He sat and thanked her as she put a plate in front of him piled high with an omelet, toast, and fried potatoes. She placed a plate with a smaller portion across from him. While gathering utensils, she reached into the refrigerator and grabbed two cans of soda and brought them to the table before sitting across from him.

"See. Not so hard," she told him with a teasing smile.

"You make it look easy," he muttered in a deep voice.

"My mom had to work a lot when I was a kid. I learned to cook pretty early in life," she explained. "She needed help around the house."

Ellie ate slowly, mostly watching Zane as he devoured the food on his plate like it was the best meal he'd ever eaten. When she'd downed all the food she could from her plate, she pushed it across the table. "I'm done. Can you finish this?"

He gave her a look of displeasure. "You didn't eat much."

"You know I can't." Ellie knew her body would fill out soon enough. She'd already put on weight, and with her slow metabolism, it wouldn't take long for her to completely fill in some of the weight she'd lost. She was determined to watch her weight and not put on the extra pounds she didn't need.

He took her plate and put it on top of his, and then quickly demolished what was left of her food.

Once finished, he refused to let her get up from the table and help him clean up.

"You cooked. I can clean. I know how to put dishes in the dishwasher," he insisted as he motioned her back into her chair.

She sat back down and watched as his big body moved efficiently around the kitchen. He might not be able to cook, but he made short work of loading the dishes and then starting the dishwasher.

Zane was tall and muscular, but he was naturally lithe, his body more like a runner's than a weightlifter's. He didn't have a spare ounce of fat anywhere on his body, which was disappointing. Ellie would have liked to see at least a tiny flaw in Zane, something to make him seem more human. But his body was sculpted, and even with a layer of scruff on his face and his dark hair a little too long, he was damn near perfect.

With a silent, inward sigh, she knew exactly why she'd always been attracted to him. Zane was perfect, but he was an enigma, a puzzle with so many pieces she'd never quite been able to put them all together. He was kind, handsome as sin, but a little bit awkward occasionally, which was endearing considering he was so damn hot in almost every other way.

As she looked around, Ellie realized he was still disorganized, but the trait was pretty much forgivable considering he was a genius. His laser focus was generally on one thing: his work.

There were things she couldn't quite understand…like why he'd kissed her. Why he was helping her when he could have turned that job over to his mother—or hers, for that matter. Ellie knew her mom would have stayed if she really needed her, but Zane had promised he'd take care of Ellie for her until she could come back for another visit. Convinced her daughter would be okay, her mom had gone back to Montana because she needed to work.

Zane's protective instincts made Ellie feel safe, but they were also perplexing. She wasn't used to having anyone who really cared about her or about what happened to her except for Chloe. He'd saved her life with his persistent nature, and Ellie was grateful, but she still didn't understand why he hadn't just given up like everyone else. Seven months was a long time.

She ran her hand through her hair, the action reminding her that she needed to cut much of it off to get it healthy again. It was pretty damaged. The thought depressed her because her long blonde hair was one of the only things she'd ever really liked about her appearance.

"What's wrong? You look sad," Zane observed as he sat back down at the table and took a slug of his soda.

"I have to cut my hair," she answered solemnly. "It's damaged, and to get it healthy again I'm going to have to cut most of it off." What had taken her years to grow out healthy and long would be gone in a matter of minutes.

Zane looked puzzled. "So just get it cut. It will grow out again."

"It's the only thing that I ever liked about how I looked. I liked my hair."

Ellie knew it wasn't really the issue of her hair that was bothering her. The whole ordeal she'd suffered was starting to hit her hard, and the loss of her hair was just a symbol of everything she'd lost. Reality was starting to close in on her.

"It's just protein filaments and dead cells, Ellie. It's just hair," he said in a husky voice.

"I know." She nodded tearfully. "It's stupid to be upset about something so superficial. I think I'm just starting to realize how much everything is going to change, how much I have to take care of and how different things will be now. I don't have a job or a home. It's like life moved on without me, but I'm still here. Now I'm trapped someplace between existing and not. I'm not sure where I go from here."

Zane stood and scooped her up from the chair and carried her into her room and laid her gently on the bed. "You need to sleep. Don't think so much. You'll end up overwhelmed. Take one thing at a time. I can't promise you that you'll feel normal again tomorrow. But I promise I'll do everything in my power to make you happy again."

"I don't feel normal," she told him breathlessly, panic beginning to set in.

Zane kicked off his boots and climbed onto the big bed, gathering her up in his arms before answering, "You'll feel normal again, Ell. I promise."

Zane's words were comforting, but her memories began to swamp her. Every one of them was frightening. Still, she started to talk. "Sometimes he made me beg for whatever food and water he'd brought with him. I was so hungry and thirsty that I didn't care if I begged. Depending on what mood he was in, sometimes it was worse than others. I always knew he'd beat me up, use me as a target for whatever anger he'd stored up while smiling at everyone else. He was evil, Zane, probably the most psychotic person I've ever met. I started to hate myself because I was so afraid, and that I gave in to everything he wanted just to get some scraps of food and water."

His arms tightened around her as he pulled her head against his chest. "Don't," he said roughly. "Don't blame yourself for anything you did to survive. Being afraid in that situation is normal. I'm not a counselor, but even I know that when you're a survivor, you do what you have to do. I fucking hate it that you ever had to be afraid, that the bastard ever laid a hand on you. If he wasn't already dead, I'd kill him myself for what he did to you and to Chloe."

Ellie took deep breaths, helping her heartbeat to calm and her panic begin to recede. She'd lived through James's captivity. Everything else was just hard work. "He was a sadistic bastard. Sociopathic. He would have eventually hurt Chloe even worse. Once I knew what he was, I was petrified that he'd actually kill her to get her money. I was so relieved to find out she didn't marry him, and that he was dead."

"He didn't just hurt her physically. He also crushed her pride and self-esteem. But she's dealing with it. I like Walker. I think he's good for her."

"I'm glad she's happy," Ellie shared.

"You'll be happy again someday, too," Zane insisted, rubbing a comforting hand down her back. "It will take time."

"You said you didn't see my car. I wonder what happened to it. He had to have hidden it or destroyed it."

"Don't worry about your car, your job, or anything else right now. You need time to heal," Zane grumbled. "We'll go to town tomorrow and get you some of the things you need. You know the police are going to want to talk to you. The asshole might be dead, but they're going to want your statement so they can close the case."

"I know," she said stoically. "I hate talking about it, but I will."

"Don't worry about anything except getting stronger. Pretty soon you'll have Chloe back, and right now you have me." His voice was stubbornly adamant.

She relaxed, leaning against his strength. There was never really a time she'd depended on anyone. She was used to being the organizer, the caretaker, even from a very young age.

For once, it was nice to have somebody to lean on.

He shifted onto his back and pulled her partially across his body, keeping her head on his chest. Threading one hand through her hair, he rubbed her back with the other in a soothing, circular motion.

"I'm tired," she admitted, feeling so emotionally and physically drained that her eyes flickered closed.

"Then sleep."

"I don't want you to leave me," she admitted, her tremulous tone vulnerable.

She didn't want to be alone with her thoughts and away from his comforting presence right now. Tomorrow, she would start growing stronger. But for right now, she needed him.

"I'm not going anywhere, Ellie. I'll be right here."

She sighed with relief and snuggled into the heat radiating from his body. "Thank you."

"Do you trust me?" Zane asked hoarsely.

"Yes."

"Then sleep. Nobody will ever hurt you again," he vowed.

He sounded so serious that she smiled, feeling safe in his powerful embrace. When she finally drifted off a few minutes later, she fell almost immediately into a deep and dreamless slumber.

When she woke up the next morning, feeling rested, Zane was gone. Ellie might have thought she'd imagined him or dreamed about him ever being there, comforting her in a tender way she'd never thought possible for Zane, but she knew she hadn't dreamed up his presence.

One deep whiff of her pillow filled her senses with his scent, proving that he'd been there in her bed, but had quietly left her to sleep.

Rolling over on her back, she tried to clear his tantalizing essence from her lungs, stop her body from reacting to the fact that he'd been in her bed, that she'd wallowed in the security of having him close.

I can't start needing him this much!

Her body and brain warred against each other as her core clenched with a primal need for the one man she'd ever really wanted.

Sitting up in bed, she swiped the hair from her face and admitted that waking up without him there beside her made her miss him, and it scared the hell out of a woman who was used to being just fine alone.

Chapter 5

Several days later, Zane was working in his underground lab, trying to figure out when Ellie Winters had become so damn stubborn. She'd been a sweet teenager, but somewhere along the way, the woman had developed an ornery, independent streak that seemed never-ending.

So I replaced some of her belongings: a cell phone, a laptop, new clothing with some help from Lara, and a few other things that she needs for everyday life. They're just essentials.

Zane didn't think what he'd done was any big deal. But he'd made Ellie emotionally upset, and he wasn't even certain why she'd been weeping when he gave her the everyday stuff. He hadn't asked why she'd cried because it made him feel sick inside that he'd been the cause of her tears. All he wanted was for Ellie to be happy, and apparently she had been making progress despite her previous tearful reaction to his gifts…until today.

Today was the day he'd realized just how obstinate Ellie could really be.

She had literally set her foot down, stomping it in refusal, when he'd brought home the new vehicle he'd acquired for her, flat-out refusing to take something he'd bought for her. She claimed it was too expensive. When he'd mentioned that she'd only had liability insurance on her missing vehicle, and that her insurance company wasn't going to pay anything to replace her piece of junk *Blue Turtle*, she'd glared at him and walked away.

"It's just a BMW. She acts like I went out and bought something really expensive. The Beemer was a reasonable choice, something solid and dependable. It's not like I went out and blew a bunch of money on an exotic sports car," Zane mumbled under his breath as he recreated some of the findings of one of his lead scientists at the lab, rechecking the results himself. "And it's an SUV. It's practical for Colorado. Plenty of people have one here."

Granted, he wanted to see some of Ellie's old spirit revived. But pissing her off wasn't exactly the way he'd wanted *that* to happen. Nevertheless, she *was* angry. But regardless of how stubborn she was going to be, Zane decided she *would* be driving a dependable car, the one *he'd* purchased for her.

After finishing his work, he input his verification into the lab computer and put away his supplies, wondering how he could get Ellie to accept the inevitable. She *was* going to use the SUV. He wanted her using a reliable vehicle. He didn't want her buying another piece of crap like her last car. It had been too small, too old, too unreliable, and all of those things were unacceptable to him.

He took off the disposable covering he was wearing over his clothing and then dumped his mask and gloves into the hazardous materials container he kept near the door.

Zane could admit he was disorganized, but only with anything *outside* of his lab. *Here*, he was meticulous. *Here*, it mattered to him. Working with potentially dangerous organisms didn't leave room for mistakes.

He washed his hands and dried them before he stood in front of the steel doors and used his fingerprint scanner to make the double doors *swoosh* open. As he walked down the hallway and up the stairs that led to the house, he contemplated his options.

Let Ellie have her way and return the BMW? *Nope. Not gonna happen. She needs a safe vehicle.*

Convince Ellie to take it? *Probably unlikely.* Though, Zane admitted she'd looked pretty mulishly insistent over not accepting his gift. He realized that he liked *that* look on her. It was preferable to seeing her weep, but it wasn't going to stop him from making sure she was driving dependable transportation.

Get Chloe to help him convince her? *A possibility, but Chloe isn't home yet, and she doesn't even know Ellie is still alive.*

Throw Ellie over his shoulder and toss her into the car? *Yep. That idea had merit since he'd been feeling like a damn protective caveman since the minute Ellie disappeared.*

Now that he'd found her, the urge to make sure Ellie was safe was almost overwhelming, a compulsive, raw instinct that he was barely managing to control.

Get it together. You'll scare her off. Hell, I'm scaring myself.

Zane considered himself a reasonable, rational, logical guy. He made decisions based on data and realistic facts. Lately, he wasn't reacting with his normal levelheadedness; he was giving in to emotions and compulsions he couldn't seem to control. He'd never experienced those types of feelings before, and it confounded him that with Ellie, he sometimes couldn't control his own words or behavior.

For some reason, Ellie had always been a woman he wanted to know better but ended up avoiding because he'd considered her off-limits in the past. However, it hadn't stopped him from asking about her when he talked to Chloe. He'd almost blown it in the hospital, letting Ellie know that, little by little, he'd gotten to know her preferences by encouraging Chloe to talk about her best friend. Zane knew Ellie's favorite was Asian food because Chloe had mentioned it. She'd also told him that she was sending Ellie her favorite chocolates for a birthday surprise a few years ago. Zane had asked what kind, and he still remembered exactly what company made the confections.

He activated the metal door to the garage hallway by using the fingerprint scanner again, and then pushed the doorway open, a hidden door that wasn't really detectable from inside the house unless one was really looking.

He strode down the hallway, but stopped short when he heard Ellie's voice. He could see her at the kitchen table with her laptop, her eyes glued to the screen as she spoke.

It took him a moment to realize what she was doing. She'd been having a video chat.

The counseling sessions!

He'd known Ellie was going to use her new laptop for sessions with a psychologist in England, but he hadn't known they were starting today. Of course, he and Ellie hadn't really had a chance to have a civil conversation this morning before he'd retreated to his lab.

He leaned against the wall and froze, not wanting to interrupt her, and shamelessly listening in on her conversation.

Unfortunately for him, they seemed to be wrapping things up.

Ellie sighed as she appeared to reply to the therapist. "Thank you, Natalie. It helped a lot to talk about how I feel. I know it's very late there for you, but I'm glad you agreed to help me."

Zane watched as Ellie said good-bye and confirmed another appointment in a few days. She closed the laptop with a pensive look on her face.

She needs to talk; she needs support.

He clenched his fists as he cursed himself for not knowing how to really talk to her. He wanted to be there, wanted to be her sounding board. He just wasn't sure exactly how to be what she needed right now.

He knew a very big part of Ellie wanted to just forget what had happened to her, just like he wished he could do. But it wasn't healthy for her to keep denying that she'd been traumatized by her seven-month ordeal. She'd never really heal if she stuffed it away inside her and never pulled it out and dealt with her emotions.

He moved into the kitchen and sat down across from her. "Do you want to talk about it? How did it go?" He hoped like hell she'd gotten over her anger from earlier that morning. He didn't want her to shut him out, even though he didn't have a fucking clue what to say.

She shook her head, but started to talk anyway. "Natalie thinks I have post-traumatic stress."

Zane raised an eyebrow. "What do you think?" He didn't know much about mental health, but he was personally willing to bet that most people who had endured what Ellie had been through were bound to suffer symptoms of post-traumatic stress.

"I suppose I probably do. I can't hear a noise that reminds me of my time as James's prisoner without getting nervous and scared. Sometimes I get flashbacks. That's why I'd rather not acknowledge it at all. But it haunts me. My life is a mess because of what happened. I feel like I've lost my independence, my entire life because of what happened. And I'm still afraid of what's going to happen to me."

"Not a fucking thing is going to happen to you, Ellie. You're home with people who care about you in this town. You're not dependent just because you need some help from friends right now. You've been through too much to deal with this alone," he told her reasonably. "Take the help I'm offering you. Your life will slowly return to normal. You just need time."

Zane could literally feel her desperation and sorrow, and it nailed him in the chest like a knife. He wanted to make everything all better for Ellie, but he felt so damn powerless. He couldn't take away her memories or the damage that fucking James had inflicted on her emotionally.

She trained her sapphire eyes on him as she answered, "That's just it. I've never *not* been able to take care of myself. Things aren't as bad as I thought they would be. Somebody has been taking care of my bills, and I have an enormous amount of money in the bank. It has to be Chloe, and I'm going to need to talk to her about it."

"It wasn't Chloe," he confessed. "It was me. I paid your bills, and I put money into your checking to cover any bills that might be on auto-pay."

She looked at him in surprise. "Why?"

Zane clenched his fists on the table. "Because I was never going to admit that you weren't coming back, and I wanted your life to be as close to normal as possible when we found you. Since you weren't here to deal with things, I did it for you. That's what friends do, right?"

He wasn't about to tell her that he'd *needed* to take care of her personal life, that he'd *needed* to do those things to convince *himself* that she *would* be back. In a way, it had been therapeutic for him, a way of convincing himself that Ellie wasn't dead. Chloe had been dealing with enough troubles of her own, and he hadn't wanted his sister to take care of Ellie's personal responsibilities. He'd wanted to do it himself.

She was silent for a few moments before she answered solemnly. "Thank you. But I'm going to have to pay you back when I get a job."

"You don't need a damn job right now. You just need to focus on getting well," he told her gruffly.

"I need to find a job, Zane. I can't handle this. I can't not want to feel normal again. For me, that means making a living." She put her face into her hands in a gesture of defeat.

Zane's heart fell to his feet. He hated seeing her this way. He wasn't used to it. Ellie was a capable, anally organized, cheerful type of woman. Seeing her all but destroyed was killing him.

"Then work for me, Ellie," he offered before he could even think about his words. "I need you. Look around this house and you'll understand why. I need a personal assistant I can trust, and that's hard to find. I need an organizer for things inside and outside of work."

She moved her hands to look at him curiously. "Don't you have an assistant?"

"No. The last one I had almost sold company secrets to one of my competitors. Luckily, we caught him in time. I haven't trusted anyone enough since then, and it happened a few years ago. We have secretaries at varying levels of security at the lab, but most of them don't have access to personal documents or research results."

She frowned. "Somebody who worked for you tried to betray you?"

It hadn't been the first time, and definitely wouldn't be the last, but Ellie didn't understand what people were willing to do for millions or billions of dollars. "I know you think I'm paranoid because everything is on tight security here, but when I'm home, I have a lot of information with me—research results and projects that some of our competitors would want for all the wrong reasons. It has to be secured."

"There has to be a ton of people who are more qualified to work for you. I don't have a college education," she argued. "I don't know anything about biotechnology."

He shrugged. "It doesn't matter. I just have to have someone I trust, someone to help me stay organized outside of the lab. I have faith in you, Ellie. If anyone can get me organized, it's you."

She looked at him for a few minutes before asking, "What would I do?"

He grinned at her, suddenly knowing exactly how he was going to get her to drive her new vehicle. "Whatever I say. The first thing you'd do is accept the car I gave you." He saw her open her mouth to protest, so he held up a hand. "You'll need a car. What if you have to run errands or do something for business?"

She glared at him, but dropped the subject. "What would my duties be?"

"Anything I want. When you're feeling better, you'll see how badly I need some organization in this house. My home in Denver is about the same, although it's cleaner thanks to my housekeeper. But she never wants to touch my personal stuff. My brain is usually so busy thinking about current projects that I don't get much else done." The more he thought about it, the more he liked the idea of Ellie taking on the job as his personal assistant. It might put him in a hell of his own making by having her around him a lot, but it was better than worrying about how she was doing all the damn time.

"Would I have to move to Denver?" she asked cautiously.

"No. When I'm there, you can stay with me. My house there is just about the same size as this one. We'll be going back and forth." Zane wanted to start spending more time in Rocky Springs. His mom wasn't getting any younger, and Rocky Springs was still home for him.

"Are you doing this because you really need me, or because you feel sorry for me?" Ellie asked bluntly.

"Believe me, I need you," Zane answered honestly, a double meaning in his words, his cock hard just from sitting across from her at a fucking kitchen table. He admitted he was desperate for her, but not in a way that he could confess to Ellie.

"Will you allow me to pay you back from my paycheck for the car and other things you've bought?"

He shook his head. "No. Those are the perks of working for a rich man. Personal assistants get personal gifts sometimes."

"Not like this," she muttered, sounding unhappy. "What's the salary? Benefits?"

Zane named a yearly salary and explained the benefits, as much as he knew anyway. He had a human resources department that dealt with that kind of thing.

"Oh, my God. That's way too much."

"It's not much more than I paid my last assistant," Zane said insistently. "And that was a few years ago." He paused before adding, "I really do need you, Ellie. After what happened, I doubt I could trust anybody else to do the job."

He held his breath as he watched her brows draw together, her expression thoughtful. Zane wondered what the hell she was thinking, but he didn't want to stop her thought process to ask.

"Okay. I'll do it. What would you like me to do first, boss?" she asked teasingly.

Zane released a long breath of relief. "I'd like you to get well and be happy," he grumbled. "No work until you feel ready."

She nodded sharply. "I'm ready."

"Smartass," he rasped.

"Zane, I'm already bored," she cajoled. "Give me something to do."

"Let's go into town. I need a haircut, and I'd like to check out the new bookstore."

Ellie ran a hand through her hair. "I need somebody to cut mine, too. I was going to do it myself, but I was afraid I'd screw it up because I can't see the back very well."

"Then let's go." He jumped up and held out his hand. Waiting.

Come on, sweetheart. Take my hand. Let me fucking help you.

"We need to go to the grocery store. I can't keep making something out of nothing. We need more food."

Zane didn't miss the flash of fear that crept across her face when she was talking about needing food supplies. Obviously, being low on food frightened her. "We'll fill up the cupboards. I promise."

He'd take her out for dinner tonight, and then they could shop for other things. Zane was pretty sure it was safe enough to go into town. Either the media had given up and moved on to a new story, or they were still camped out at the hospital in Denver.

Tate had mentioned he'd taken care of the problem, and Zane hadn't asked any questions. Knowing his youngest brother, he'd created a good story, and had steered everyone away from Rocky Springs somehow.

Zane nearly groaned with pleasure as Ellie placed her smaller hand into his and let him pull her to her feet. The way she trusted him floored him after all she'd been through.

As his engorged cock threatened to separate the zipper of his jeans, Zane knew that if the touch of her hand in his got him this hard, it was going to be a very long evening.

Chapter 6

E llie was exhausted as she walked down Main Street in Rocky Springs, tugging at her new short, curly haircut. Her hair had always been just a little bit wavy, but cut in a style that barely touched her shoulders instead of her lower spine, the big curls were now more pronounced.

She smiled as she looked into the window of a local clothing store, remembering how Zane had supported her by going into the salon with her. He'd even gotten his own hair cut right there beside her, and the shorter style suited him.

Like he's not hot enough?

The hairstylist had clipped him short, and it made those Colter gray eyes pop, making them even more expressive.

"And I look like a poodle," she mumbled to herself as she let the curl she was fingering spring back into place. The style was fine, but without the length, she thought her hair did rather resemble that of the curly-haired canine.

Still, her heart ached with gratitude that Zane had been kind enough to sit right next to her as the stylist clipped off all of her fuzzy, damaged hair.

It's just hair.

Zane was right, of course. Ellie wasn't vain, and it wasn't the loss of her only decent physical asset that she was mourning. It was admitting that the toll of the entire months-long ordeal was getting to her now that she was physically healing.

She sighed as she pulled open the door of the clothing store, remembering Zane's demanding parting words as he'd walked across the street to check out the bookstore while she went to buy a few more clothing essentials after they'd gotten groceries and loaded them into his SUV.

Don't leave the store without everything you want.

Of course she *wouldn't* buy everything she *wanted*. She never did. Ellie lived on a tight budget, but she had almost everything she needed to get by for a while. Thanks to Zane, she had more money in her bank account than she'd ever seen before. Her future plan was to take an accounting of what she owed him and work it off while she worked for him. Unfortunately, he wasn't about to tell her exactly what he'd spent, but she could work the numbers out fairly accurately.

Her spirits lifted as she thought about working for Zane, learning new things as his assistant. She wanted to just be a sponge and suck up as much information as she possibly could about biotechnology. Ellie wanted to be an asset to Zane, and she knew she could be, especially if it required organization—something he desperately needed and one skill that she had where she definitely excelled.

As she walked through the door, she literally collided with a woman who was hurrying toward the exit.

"Oh, I'm sorry," Ellie apologized.

"My fault. I'm always in a hurry," the petite woman answered, breathless. She paused for a moment before she added, "Ellie?"

It was her previous landlady who owned her old apartment building. "Hello, Gina."

"Oh, my God. I can't believe it," Gina squealed, hugging Ellie tightly before stepping back. "You look…"

"Tired?" Ellie suggested, feeling wiped out and knowing her body was so unused to physical activity that it would take a while to build her stamina up again.

"No, no, no," Gina denied. "You look good. Just different."

Probably because I'm skinny and I have hair like a poodle.

"Getting kidnapped can change a person," Ellie joked, still not knowing how to respond to people who looked at her like she was a ghost. She'd lived in Rocky Springs all her life, and she knew a whole lot of the residents. It seemed strange that they looked at her like she'd come back from the dead. Well, maybe they were mostly right.

"You look good." Gina smiled at her.

"I'm sorry you had to evict me. You lost money on my apartment. I'd like to repay you."

Gina look stunned. "I didn't lose money, and I never evicted you. Everything was paid every month by one of the Colter boys. The scientist. He just had your things removed a little while back, when he found you alive." She dug around in her purse and handed Ellie an envelope. "The apartment was in amazing condition. Thank you for getting it cleaned. This is your deposit. I made it out, but I wasn't sure where to send it."

Ellie took the check distractedly, shoving it into the pocket of her jacket. "So you never had to store my stuff? My rent was always paid on time?"

"Of course," Gina answered earnestly. "And I never would have evicted you until I knew what had happened. I knew disappearing wasn't like you. I knew something bad had happened."

This means that Zane lied. But why?

"Thank you," Ellie replied awkwardly.

Gina patted her cheek. "You're very welcome. Let me know if there's anything I can do to help you."

Ellie watched as Gina turned and pulled open the door.

"Gina?" she called impulsively. "Did you rent my apartment out again?"

The other woman smiled. "Somebody just signed a lease today."

Today? It wasn't rented before? Another lie?

Ellie tried to smile as she called to the exiting woman. "Thank you."

Gina waved as she rushed out the door.

Ellie was confused, her mind filled with questions. *Why had Zane lied about her apartment already being rented? Why hadn't he told her that he'd paid the rent every month? Why hadn't he let her go back to her own apartment?*

It was clear that her staying with him was no accident. Zane had set it up to be that way. He'd made sure she had absolutely no option but to stay with him.

She was angry, furious that he hadn't been completely honest with her. Feeling conflicted because he'd taken such good care of her, Ellie went to find some clothing, hoping that Zane had a damn good explanation.

"I know you're a damn genius, but do you really need that many books?"

Zane froze as he heard his brother Tate's sarcastic voice right behind him. Hefting the books to his chest so his brother couldn't see what they were, he turned slowly, realizing it wasn't just Tate in the bookstore. Blake, Tate, and Marcus were all looking at him questioningly.

"I happen to enjoy reading. Unlike the rest of you, I like to keep my brain active," he answered defensively. "What in the hell are you all doing here anyway?"

"Lara is coming home late from school, and Mom isn't around tonight either, so we all went to get something to eat," Tate confessed.

Zane smirked, knowing not a single one of his brothers could cook worth a damn…just like him. Their mother had spoiled every one of them by being a Betty Crocker clone. There was never a moment during their childhood when their mother hadn't cooked like a fiend because she loved doing it. Still did. And Zane took advantage of the fact that his mother liked to cook as often as possible. He knew when his brothers were home; they conveniently sought her out at dinnertime, too.

Tate removed the books from Zane's grasp before he could stop him, pissed off as his brother looked at the titles.

"Every one of these is a relationship book," Tate said slowly, his eyebrow lifting as he perused the heavy one on how to romance a woman.

"Yeah? So what?" Zane snatched the books back angrily.

"I didn't know you were seeing someone," Blake said, sounding slightly wounded.

"I'm not," Zane admitted.

"Then what's with the books?" Marcus questioned curiously.

Zane would be damned if he'd let his brothers make him feel ridiculous because he wanted self-help books. At least *he* knew he needed help. Tate had been damn lucky to score a wife like Lara, and Blake and Marcus were too busy with work to worry about doing anything but screw a woman when they felt the need.

Blake thumbed through another stack on the table right beside Zane. "These yours too?" He paused before adding, "These are different—books on psychology: post-traumatic stress, emotional healing after trauma, and coping with post-traumatic stress."

"Ellie?" Marcus guessed. "How is she doing?"

Zane could tell that Tate would have liked to keep poking at him, something the brothers did a lot, but Marcus's question silenced his youngest brother.

Zane shrugged. "She's doing as well as she can be considering she was beaten, held captive for months in a shithole, wondering what day James would decide to kill her, and being nearly starved to death."

"Are you getting involved with her, Zane?" Tate asked in a more serious tone. "I'm all for her staying with you where she's safe. I even helped make that happen. But she isn't heal—"

"No," Zane told his brother adamantly. "We *aren't* involved. She's my friend. I want to understand her. I want to help her," he replied, his tone edgy, wishing to hell that was all he wanted from Ellie. But he'd be lying to himself. He wanted more someday, but mostly he wanted her to be happy.

"You did help," Marcus answered reasonably. "You saved her life. You're the only one who didn't give up on her except Chloe. Still a damn miracle that she's alive, if you ask me."

"I didn't ask," Zane answered irritably. "I don't want to talk about Ellie. She's been through enough."

"You like her. If you don't, then I have to wonder about your choice of reading material," Blake remarked with a smile.

Honestly, Zane hadn't planned on getting so many books. But every one of them had jumped out at him as he looked through the small bookstore. "I want to understand her," he snapped at his brothers. "I want to know what she went through, and I want to help her get through all of this. She lost her whole goddamn life, and it isn't fair. All because of some bastard who just happened to cross her path."

"She's not going to heal overnight, Zane," Blake warned. "It could take a while before she even feels partially normal again."

Slamming the books down on the table next to the psychology books he'd selected, he crossed his arms and faced his brother. "I don't care how long it takes. I'll be there for her."

"She might not be ready for a relationship right now, Zane. You saved her life and she's going to be grateful," Tate mused. "Her emotions are going to get all tangled up. Right now, you're her hero."

Zane knew his brothers were trying to protect him, but it irritated the crap out of him that they were insinuating that Ellie could never genuinely like him. "I'm not looking for a relationship right now. I'm just trying to right a wrong for a friend."

"Then what's with the books?" Marcus leaned his hip against the table and folded his arms in front of him. "Planning on meeting the woman of your dreams shortly?"

"Why is that any of your business?" Zane growled, not about to admit that he wanted Ellie to have the things she'd never experienced and never had. *He* wanted to be the man to make her feel alive again. Except he didn't know a damn thing about romancing a woman. "I'm a science geek who spends all of his time in a lab. Maybe I need to learn something about women."

"Just care about her like you've been doing. That's all you really have to do," Tate answered huskily, his tone making it obvious that he was thinking about his wife.

"It's not that simple," Zane argued in a raspy voice, wanting to make them understand, as if they could actually help him. "I care about Ellie. I always have. But I want more than I've had with her before. I want *her* more than I ever have before. Or maybe the feelings have always been there, and I just saw her as off-limits because she was Chloe's best friend. Now, I wish I had pursued her once we were both adults. Maybe this never would have happened to her. Do you know she's never experienced anything remotely romantic from a guy? What in the hell is wrong with men in this town? She deserves romance. It's something she's never experienced, and apparently something most women dream about. I want to give her everything she wants. Fuck! I know it's too soon, but eventually I guess I'm hoping..." His voice trailed off, not sure what else to say. Hell, he didn't even understand his actions himself. All he knew was his compulsion to make Ellie smile again, laugh again.

Zane watched as his brothers all looked at one another before turning back to him. "You're screwed," Tate told him simply.

Blake and Marcus nodded in agreement, their expressions grim.

"Why?" Zane felt compelled to ask.

Tate shrugged. "You'll figure it out when Ellie becomes all you can think about, an obsession that you can't control. When you start worrying about her safety and whether or not she's happy because you're positive that you can't live without her."

"I'm already there," he answered morosely, knowing his youngest brother had the most experience with relationships since he was the only married brother. "I don't know much about what happened during her months in captivity. Sometimes I don't even want to think about it because I'm afraid I'll lose it. Hell, I even have nightmares about it sometimes, and I wasn't even there. I'm pissed off as hell because she didn't deserve what happened, and I can't even kill James for hurting her because he's already dead."

"I'd feel the same way, bro," Tate admitted. "When Lara sacrificed herself to a terrorist to save my life, I lost it when he touched her. I get it. But Lara didn't go through what Ellie did. She didn't spend months in captivity being treated like she wasn't human. I'm not sure I could handle that without losing my mind. But she's going to need to talk about it. She's going to need to get through it before she can focus on a real relationship. I know this doesn't help much, but just be there for her."

"She needs time," Blake stated bluntly. "Is she getting therapy?"

Zane nodded. "The same one that Chloe uses. Dr. Townson thinks Ellie has post-traumatic stress. Dammit! I don't want her to have to be afraid anymore. It's over."

Marcus nodded. "PTSD makes sense. Zane, a person can't go through a prolonged period of confinement like that without some damage to her psyche."

"She's handling it well. Really well," Zane explained. "Better than most people would. But sometimes I can see the fear in her eyes, and it's fucking killing me." If someone put him in a lab, he was in his element. Outside of work, he was like a fish out of water. He didn't know what to say or do to help Ellie heal.

"Then just keep being supportive," Blake suggested. "Give her time."

"Spoken like a guy who has never wanted a woman so desperately that he'd do anything to have her," Tate mumbled. "If you want a real relationship with a woman who makes you crazy, things get complicated."

Things were *beyond* complicated for Zane. And he wanted nothing more than to claim Ellie in the most elemental way possible. Yet, he also wanted her to feel safe. How in the hell did a man deal with those two conflicting emotions: rampant desire and protectiveness? In his mind, a guy either wanted to fuck a woman or he wanted to protect her—like he wanted to protect his younger sister, Chloe. For him, those two emotions had never co-existed before.

"I'll deal with it," Zane told his brothers, trying hard to sound a hell of a lot more confident about the situation than he really was.

Tate snorted as Zane gathered up his books to go pay for them. "That's what I said when my dick got hard every time I looked at Lara."

Zane made his way to the checkout, but his brothers trailed closely behind him. "Lara is the best thing that ever happened to you," Zane answered gruffly, knowing he'd give anything to have what Tate had: a woman who loved him even with all of his faults.

Tate shrugged. "I'd never deny that." His voice was unwavering. "But it can be hell before the honeymoon starts."

Zane handed the cashier money, waving at her to keep the change as he gathered up the bags of books. Turning to leave and glaring at his brothers as he muscled his way in between them, he informed them, "There isn't going to be a honeymoon. Christ! I just want to help her right now, okay? She went through hell and back. Ellie needs somebody right now."

"Do you want me to take her in for a while?" Blake asked blandly. "I wouldn't mind having her as my guest. I've always liked Ellie, and I have plenty of room at the ranch."

"I wouldn't mind helping either." Marcus echoed his twin's offer. "I'll be around for the holidays."

Zane saw red at the thought of Ellie being with any other man but him, even his brothers. They wouldn't care about her the same way he did. "Hell, no. And if either of you offer, I'll make you regret it," he told them ominously before he made his way around them and promptly exited the bookstore without ever looking back.

The other three Colter brothers gave one another a questioning look.

"He really is screwed," Tate said solemnly. "Shit! I want him to be happy, but he could be looking at a pretty bumpy road. Ellie's confused. She isn't going to know what she wants until she's had some time and counseling."

Blake nodded slowly. "Zane will give her time. He'll do what's best for Ellie."

"Are the two of you blind? She's perfect for him," Marcus drawled. "She always has been. The timing just sucks."

Tate looked at Marcus with surprise. "How do you know she's the one for Zane?"

Marcus rolled his eyes. "Observation. The few times I've seen them together since Zane left Rocky Springs, it's been pretty obvious. I've seen the way they look at each other. I don't doubt that Ellie has genuine feelings for Zane. It's not a bad case of hero worship. She's always liked him. He's always liked her. I'm surprised he's never gone after her before. Maybe it was because she was Chloe's best friend. I don't think he realized just how much he wanted her until she disappeared."

"What if you're wrong?" Blake asked gruffly.

Marcus looked at both of his brothers for a moment before answering with a certainty that came out sounding very much like arrogance. "I'm never wrong."

Tate and Blake watched as Marcus turned and walked toward the exit, his declaration still hanging in the air. The two of them just shook their heads and eventually followed behind him, neither one of them able to think of a single smartass thing to say.

Chapter 7

Zane stowed his heavy load of books in the car before he crossed the street in search of Ellie. Not that he was ashamed of what he'd purchased, but it would probably bring up questions that he didn't want to, and couldn't, answer right now.

Gut instinct was driving him to learn about what Ellie had gone through, and he wanted to understand the trauma she'd experienced. He felt so damn hopeless when it came to comforting the beautiful woman who needed reassurance. Problem was, he'd never been a romantic type of guy, and he sure as hell had never had female friends who had been through what Ellie had experienced.

Maybe I should have called Chloe back home.

He shook his head as he walked to the clothing store, knowing his little sister was going to be pissed. But all in all…he agreed with Ellie. Chloe had her own issues to resolve and she deserved her time away. No doubt she *would* feel guilty about Ellie being in bad shape from the kidnapping. Zane knew that Blake had probably already told Gabe. Blake and Chloe's husband had been best friends for a long time. Obviously, Gabe had felt it was better to wait until Chloe came home or Zane knew his little sister would already be back from her travels. There would have been no way to keep Chloe away from Rocky Springs if she knew that Ellie had been found alive.

Zane respected that Ellie wanted time before she saw Chloe. It really was her decision to make. He'd done enough underhanded things to force her to accept some help. He had to draw the line at directly going against her decision.

Moving a little faster, Zane shoved his hands in the pockets of his down jacket. It was after dark and it was damn cold, a light snow beginning to fall.

He stopped short as he saw Ellie in front of the clothing store, feeling like somebody had nailed him in the gut.

What. The. Hell?

Ellie looked terrified. A mobile camera crew and reporter were right in front of her, light blasting her in the face. She didn't speak. Instead, she just kept shaking her head.

Zane could only see the back of the male reporter, but as his eyes scanned the street, he could see a van with the logo of a local television station.

As he stepped forward, his jaw clenched, he knew he was going to make it physically impossible for this particular reporter to bother Ellie anytime soon.

"Fuck!" he rasped, watching as Ellie pushed her way through the gathering crowd and bolted…straight toward him.

He caught her easily, stepping into her path so her body would come to a stop when she ran into him. Wrapping his arms around her, he kept her imprisoned in his hold.

"Zane," she acknowledged tearfully. "I'm sorry. I can't talk to them right now. I don't want to remember. I don't want to talk about what happened." Her voice was panicked and frightened, a voice he'd never heard from her before.

"You don't have to," he crooned, stroking a hand over her head.

"Ms. Winters," the low, male voice of the reporter said insistently. "Just a couple of questions." The young reporter had made his way over to Ellie, the camera and light following.

"I can't," Ellie sobbed. "I can't do it right now."

Zane felt a rage start to rise, an emotion he'd never experienced before with so much intensity. "Turn off the goddamn camera," he informed the television crew. "No interviews." His voice was more of a growl as he spoke, his instinct to protect Ellie from anything that upset her impossible for him to ignore.

Eying the reporter angrily, Zane demanded, "Leave. Take your ass back to Denver or I'll make sure you can't ever do an interview again. Ellie has been through enough." *Jesus, he hated these bloodsuckers.* Reporters just kept digging until their victim practically bled out from the wounds.

"It's not like we're on your property," the reporter replied snidely. "We're totally within our rights to report the news."

Zane lost his temper. "You're not fucking reporting news. You're upsetting a victim, a woman who has been through one hell of an ordeal for no reason, through no fault of her own. The perpetrator is dead. You just want this story to entertain the curious who want to know the details." He stopped and took a long breath. "Just get the hell out of Rocky Springs and don't come back."

"You can't make me leave," the newsman responded.

"He appears to have his arms full. But if he can't make you leave, I can," a baritone drawled from behind Zane.

It was Marcus. Although Blake and Marcus sounded very similar, the smooth assurance was all Zane's eldest brother.

"Want me to hold him?" Blake questioned.

"I'll help," Tate offered angrily. "Shit! I thought I'd covered your trail so well that nobody would find her. I'm sorry, Ellie."

Zane desperately wanted to stay so he could slam the insistent reporter against a wall somewhere and shut him up, but Ellie was shivering in his arms. "Let's get you to the car." Turning, he put an arm protectively around Ellie and urged her toward his SUV parked down the street.

"We'll handle this," Marcus said stoically as Zane and Ellie passed him.

Zane nodded at him. "I know. Thanks." His brothers would make sure the media left town, no matter what it took to make that happen.

Ellie lifted her fingers to swipe away her tears aggressively. "I'm sorry. It was silly of me to get so upset over a reporter."

"It's not silly," Zane retorted. "If you're not ready, you don't have to talk about it. If you're never ready, you never have to say anything about it."

Ellie had met with the police, and she'd given a statement. But with the guilty party dead, they'd taken her brief explanation without the details and closed the case. Zane had been relieved even though he knew someday she'd have to chase away her demons by talking about it.

Maybe she'll talk to Chloe.

Zane stared down at her profile as they walked, noting that she looked exhausted. As they arrived at his vehicle, he felt guilty for not taking the bags she held. In his thirst for blood flowing from the reporter who had accosted Ellie, he hadn't noticed them. Not that it looked like she bought much. She only had two small bags.

"I'll take those. Jump in." He took her packages and opened the door for her before he went to the cargo area and stored her stuff.

Sliding into the driver's seat, he closed the door and started the car so it would warm up.

Ellie was trying to brush the snow out of her hair with her cold fingers.

"I hope you bought some more winter stuff," he grumbled as he pulled away from the curb, not even bothering to look behind him. Zane had faith that his brothers would handle the reporter situation.

"I have some winter things in my belongings. I just haven't sorted everything out yet," she said hesitantly, obviously still emotional. "I have the stuff you got me, but I didn't think I'd be outside for long." She took a deep breath. "I'm sorry for the emotional scene."

"Those people scared you?" Zane asked, his fingers tightening around the steering wheel, pissed off at anybody who caused Ellie to get upset.

"Not scared really," Ellie said with a sigh. "I just don't really want to reveal my humiliation to the entire world. I don't know if I'll ever be ready to do that."

Ellie felt shame, and that nearly pushed Zane over the edge. "It wasn't your fault. None of it was your fault."

"But that doesn't make it less humiliating," Ellie countered.

As he turned a corner to head back toward his house, he mumbled a curse before answering. James had been a psychopath, and he still remembered her briefly telling him how he'd made her beg for food and water. "Don't even feel ashamed," he said gruffly. "James was the sociopath and you were his victim. It takes a lot of courage to survive what you did, Ell."

"I let him toy with me. I let him mess with my head," Ellie answered sadly. "I knew what he was doing, and I gave him exactly what he wanted."

"What choice did you have?" Zane snapped back at her.

She didn't answer, and the long, drawn-out silence made him realize she'd had no choice. All of her freedom, respect, and dignity had been sucked out of her by a crazy asshole who liked to torment women.

He was relieved when she finally answered quietly, "None. Not a single choice. It was either die or stay alive. The survivor in me refused to give up."

"Thank fuck," Zane said huskily. "I would have been pretty irritated if I had shown up at the cabin and you were already dead."

Ellie laughed, a sound that hit Zane solidly right in the chest. He hadn't heard Ellie laugh in a long time. If his black sense of humor made her smile, he'd gladly stop trying to be politically correct.

"I'm glad I didn't disappoint you," Ellie shot back with a snort.

Zane smiled just a little as they entered Colter land and he moved toward his home. "I'm sorry I let a reporter have the opportunity to talk to you. I'm supposed to be keeping you safe."

"You do. And it wasn't your fault," Ellie argued. "Zane, you can't protect me from the world forever, no matter how much I appreciate that you try."

"The hell I can't," he shot back at her. He'd slipped up, let his brothers disrupt his visual on where she was. From now on, she'd stay safe.

"I fear it, too," Ellie said softly.

"What?" Zane questioned, wanting to know whatever the hell she feared so he could make it go away.

Silence stretched on as Zane drove across Colter property, the darkness of the night preventing him from seeing Ellie's expression.

Finally, he urged, "Talk to me, Ellie. What are you afraid of?"

"I'm afraid it will happen again," she admitted in a rush. "I know the chances of being kidnapped again, especially since James is dead, are almost nonexistent. Rationally, I understand that. But I can't stop the anxiety I feel when someone approaches me, even in a non-threatening way. If it's somebody I don't recognize as a friend, I have a knee-jerk reaction to run. Until recently, I seemed to have the same reaction even if it was a friend—just not as strong as when it's a stranger." She took a deep, tremulous breath and continued. "I know it doesn't make any sense. I knew that guy was a reporter. But when he got in my face and wanted me to talk about my experience, it was like it was going to happen all over again."

Zane's frustration with the reporter returned. "He was a pushy asshole, Ell. And you have every right to be cautious. Hell, I think you're incredibly brave just to go out of the house again."

"I want to. I can't live in fear, Zane," Ellie insisted. "I want to feel normal again. This is my town. This is where I grew up. Nothing traumatic has ever happened to me here before…" Her voice trailed off, sounding like she was afraid to mention the only devastating event she'd ever experienced in Rocky Springs.

Zane reached out in the dark, searching for contact with Ellie, hating the fact that she was essentially suffering alone. He didn't know the first thing about how to deal with her fear…or his own agitation about her safety.

Their hands connected, and his heart sank as she flinched away from him for an instant, but then she reached out and curled her fingers around his trustingly. Zane felt an aching tenderness in his chest as Ellie tightened her grip, letting him know without words that she trusted him, that her initial reaction was just a momentary, instinctive thing.

After a few minutes of silence, Ellie asked, "Why didn't you tell me that you took care of my apartment? You lied to me when you told me it was already rented."

He told her the truth because she deserved it. "I wanted your place to be waiting for you. I wanted your life to be as normal as possible when you got back. I didn't know I'd find you nearly dead. When you started refusing to come home to recover with me, I gave up your place so you had to be with me. I know it was a shitty thing to do, and I'm sorry I lied. But I'm not sorry that you're with me where you belong. Right now, I *need* you to be with me as much as you need someone to be with you so you're safe and not alone." *Christ! He was downright desperate to watch her every single moment.*

"Why?"

"Because I need the reassurance that you're fucking really alive and getting better," he told her reluctantly. "This whole thing—your disappearance, the long search, the endless days of wondering where you were and what the hell had happened to you, wondering if you were dead or alive—it all scared the hell out of me, and even though I know you're alive, the fear hasn't gone away." Zane was starting to wonder whether it ever would.

She was quiet for a moment before she finally answered, "I think you're right. I think right now I do need to be with you. Tonight proved that to me. Until I can conquer all my demons, I need you to slay them for me. I know what you did was out of fear, and Lord knows I understand that. But please don't ever lie to me, or try to manipulate me again."

That moment was pivotal for Zane. It was the instant that he knew that he was utterly and completely screwed. "I won't." He cared about her way too much not to try to keep that promise.

Chapter 8

The holidays flew by, and after a few months, she and Zane fell into a routine. He'd work in his lab during the day, but he'd show up by dinnertime. She cooked, and had slowly organized his entire house except for his lab.

Zane couldn't find anything, which she found pretty amusing. Not that he'd been very good at finding things *before* she'd organized, but when she was done, he was completely lost.

Ellie slowly started working on her aromatherapy business again, making candles and scents that made her happy. Her Internet sales weren't miraculous, but it was enough to pay for her hobby with a little left over.

Eventually, she'd gotten used to driving the BMW Zane had gifted to her, even though she thought it was ridiculous for a woman like her to be driving any kind of luxury vehicle. Slowly, she'd desensitized herself, feeling less and less afraid to be out and about, even when Zane wasn't around. With Dr. Townson's help, she was inching closer to a normal life, but she knew it was going to be a while before she was completely recovered…if she ever did.

Her body was filling out, and she'd already had to go buy a few new clothes. Hopefully, she'd reach a point where she didn't feel like she was starving all the time. Unfortunately, she hadn't gotten to that particular stage yet. Having been deprived of food for so long, Ellie acknowledged unhappily that she was making up for lost meals.

Maybe that was why she was currently munching on an enormous plate of nachos at two a.m. Having been awakened by a nightmare, one of many of the side effects of her traumatic experience, she hadn't been able to go back to sleep. She'd gotten up and turned on all the lights to chase away the shadows once she reached the kitchen, not wanting to disturb Zane with her insomnia by turning on lights in the hallway. Then, she'd promptly went to work on making an enormous batch of nachos. No doubt she'd pay for it with heartburn later, but she'd topped them off with a very liberal amount of jalapenos and salsa.

Now, she was at the other end of the enormous house, kicking back in the family room, eating nachos and focused on one of her favorite crime shows. Lucky for her, Zane had on-demand television, so whenever she had a chance, she caught up on her forensic true crime stories.

"It's not the husband," she said to the television irritably as she watched the police go down the wrong trail to find a woman's murderer. "There's no motive, no life insurance, and his grief wasn't fake," Ellie concluded, shoving more nachos into her mouth.

"What the hell are you doing?" A loud baritone boomed over the sound of the television.

Ellie squealed, almost upsetting the bowl of nachos on her lap as she turned to look at Zane. "Oh, God. I'm so sorry. I didn't think you'd be able to hear the TV."

Frantically, she glanced around for the controller so she could turn the show off. She couldn't find it. Setting the bowl down on the table in front of the couch, Ellie started feeling down the cracks in the couch.

"Ellie…stop," Zane grumbled, grabbing her by the shoulders. "You didn't wake me, and the TV didn't bother me. I woke up on my own and went to the kitchen for something to drink. I just wondered what the hell you were doing up. You went to bed early."

She breathed a sigh of relief as she looked up at him, her heart skipping a beat as she met his confused gaze. "I had a bad dream. I couldn't go back to sleep. It happens sometimes, and I know I'm not going to get back to sleep quickly, so I just get up and watch some TV."

He nodded as if he understood and then plopped down on the couch, snatched her nachos, and pulled her back down beside him. "What are we watching?"

Ellie loved the way that Zane just accepted whatever she was doing as normal and joined her in her insanity.

"True forensic cases," she answered breathlessly, her eyes unable to stay away from his muscular bare chest.

Zane might amuse her at times, but mostly, he made her entire body ache to get closer to him. He looked perfectly comfortable dressed in only a pair of flannel pajama bottoms. Ellie was fairly certain no guy looked as edible as Zane right now. His hair was artfully mussed, like he just crawled out of bed, which he had. But no man should look that good with bedhead. She thought it was completely unfair.

Ellie combed her fingers through her hair, knowing she had errant locks sticking out all over the place. Between that and a highly unsexy pair of Tinker Bell pajamas she had tugged on at bedtime, she was pretty sure she looked downright scary.

Strangely, Zane didn't seem to notice or care if she was a mess.

She snuck a sideways look at him, but he was focusing on the show now, one of his brows rising in the adorable way that happened when he was concentrating.

"You're right," Zane said as he shoved more food in his mouth, and then reached for her soda on the table and took a slug. "It's not the husband."

Ellie relaxed and leaned her back against the couch. "I know I'm right." She reached out and grabbed her soda. "He didn't have any reason to kill her."

Zane shook his head. "It's not just that. The forensic evidence doesn't implicate him. They need to move on and look for the real killer."

Ellie reached for a chip as she answered, "They will. But they always seem to need to clear the husband or boyfriend first on this show."

"You mean there are more of these types of programs?" he asked curiously.

Ellie laughed. "Tons of them, and I've watched them all. I'm an addict. I've slowly been catching up on the episodes I missed."

Getting comfortable, Zane sat through two more episodes, the two of them bantering back and forth about who committed the featured crime. Ellie was right both times, but he agreed with her in both episodes.

As the second show ended, Ellie stood up and took the empty bowl and soda can to the kitchen. After flipping off the television, Zane followed.

"Are you going to be okay now?" he asked quietly as he leaned a hip against the kitchen counter.

"I'll be fine. It's not the first time I've had a forensic marathon when I couldn't sleep," she confessed, smiling at him.

"Why didn't you wake me? I would have sat with you before tonight. You don't need to be alone."

Ellie shook her head. "I didn't want to disturb you. It's my strange little issue. I eventually go back to bed."

Truthfully, there had been nothing she wanted more than Zane's company on those sleepless nights, but it was safer for her to just sit it out alone. He was her boss now, and she needed her job. Somehow, she needed to get over her desire to climb up his ripped body like a mountaineer and ride him hard on the way back down.

"Next time…wake me up," he demanded, slowly backing her against the kitchen counter.

His body surged into hers, and Ellie could barely crane her head back enough to look at him. "Why?" she asked simply.

"Because I'll try to make you forget all your bad dreams."

"How?"

Zane's eyes flashed like molten silver, making Ellie's heart start to gallop.

Kiss me. Please kiss me.

She'd yearned to have him devour her like he had the day he'd brought her home. Only now, she never wanted him to stop. She'd become so connected to him in every way but the physical, and she yearned for that, too.

He leaned down, so close that she could feel his warm breath on the side of her face, his breathing so fast and harsh she could actually hear him.

"Fuck! I can't do this!" Zane growled as he smashed his fist against the counter beside her. "You need a friend right now. The last thing you need is a man who wants to fuck you so damn much that his balls are blue."

Ellie wrapped her arms around his neck as he went to pull back from her, stunned by Zane's confession. "You want…me?"

He nodded slowly. "I don't *want* to want you, but damned if I don't. I *shouldn't* want you because you're my friend, now my employee, and you're healing from an emotional trauma most people can't even understand. I can keep bullshitting myself forever, but I can't change what is and probably always will be. I can't rationalize it or make it make sense. But I want to bury my cock inside you and lose myself in that pleasure more than I want to take another breath." He speared a hand into her hair and fisted some of the locks. "I want to hear your moans of pleasure; hear you scream my name when you come. I want to be the next man to fuck you until you don't even know your own name."

His voice was dangerously graveled and rough, as though every word he spoke was being dragged from some deep cavern inside him. Ellie shivered as he pushed his hard body against hers, the feel of his engorged cock brushing against her pelvis. "You'd be the only man," she whispered softly, right before Zane swooped down and captured her mouth with his.

He plundered her mouth like she was his sustenance and he was starving. Ellie felt her core clench as their tongues tangled together, both of them desperately trying to get closer. As she tangled her hands in his hair, she struggled for breath as Zane nibbled on her bottom lips before soothing it with his mouth again.

"I want you, too," Ellie confessed as she buried her face in his neck, nearly sobbing as she inhaled Zane's masculine scent. "So much it hurts."

His hands strayed down her body, one landing on her ass as the other slid down the front of her ragged pajamas and under her panties. "Jesus, you're so wet for me, Ellie, and so damn hot. Do you have any idea how hard it is not to fuck you?"

She felt like she was incinerating, her entire body jerking as Zane searched and found the sensitive bundle of nerves, his thumb sliding easily around and over it because the area was so slick with moisture.

"Zane!" she cried out, her body humming with pleasure.

"Come for me, Ell. I can't fuck you because you're a virgin, but I need to see you come," he rasped right beside her ear before flicking his tongue over the sensitive skin of her neck.

Gasping as his fingers invaded her pussy, making her feel things she'd never felt before, Ellie tightened her hold on his hair and yanked until he finally yielded and kissed her, his mouth ravenous as he continued to torment her with his fingers and his wicked tongue.

The urge to crawl inside him grew stronger, and all Ellie could do was helplessly whimper against Zane's lips while she lost every thought in her head except *him* and what he was doing to her body.

Without thinking, she hopped up and wrapped her legs around his waist, almost begging for him to replace his fingers with his cock.

"I need more," Ellie begged.

"I don't think so, baby. I think you just need to come," Zane demanded, his fingers still working her clit as she pushed her hips hard against his palm.

Ellie moaned as the knot in her belly began to unfurl, the sensation going straight to her core. Holding onto Zane for dear life, she let her body take control, unable to do anything but allow him to push her over the edge.

Her entire body quivered as she flew apart, hands still clenching Zane's hair as she screamed his name. "*Zane*. Oh, God. I've never felt like this before."

"Just ride your climax," Zane commanded. "I'm here. I'll keep you safe, Ell. I promise."

She trusted him as her body bucked in pleasure. Zane moved his hands and let her use his muscular abs to rock her hips against him as she rode out the most incredible orgasm she'd ever experienced.

Her hands moved down to stroke over his back, her nails digging into his skin as she held on tight, her hips surging against him as she moaned with unbridled pleasure as her climax peaked, and she began to float back to Earth again.

Forcing her hands to relax so she didn't scratch up his bare back any more than she already had, she let her head drop on his shoulder, her body completely spent.

As she slowly lowered her legs to the floor, Zane scooped her up and carried her back to her bed.

Ellie was mute, her body and mind still shaken up. What the hell could she say? *Um…sorry I just climaxed while I humped your perfect body?* Nope. That probably wasn't the correct thing to say in this awkward situation.

Zane stroked her hair as he tucked the sheet and comforter around her. "Can you sleep now?"

Ellie stifled a yawn. "Yes."

He sat down on the bed. "Ellie, why didn't you ever tell me you were a virgin?"

"It never came up in conversation," she answered defensively. The state of her cherry was personal. It wasn't like they exactly had deep, intimate conversations about sex. In fact, it was the one thing they generally never discussed.

"I'm glad you told me before it was too late. You must be saving yourself for someone."

Her heart sank. "I guess you don't do virgins?" she asked curiously.

"No," he answered enigmatically. "Get some sleep."

He stood and clicked off the dim light from the bedside lamp before striding to the bedroom door. Turning, he said matter-of-factly, "I have to go back to Denver tomorrow for a charity ball because it's hosted by Colter Labs, and then I'm staying in the city for a while to work on some stuff at the lab. Will you go?"

Ellie swallowed hard, confused by his rejection which was then followed with him asking her to go with him to Denver. "Of course. I'm your assistant."

"I'm not asking you as an employee to accompany me to the ball," he said ominously. "I'm asking you to be my date. Will you go?"

Her heart lifted, but she still didn't know what to make of Zane's behavior. It was dark, and she couldn't see his expression. "Yes," she answered softly. "I'd love to go. I've never been to a ball."

Maybe that made her sound pathetic, but it was the truth. Chloe's mom had hosted events at her resort, and Ellie was always invited, but she'd never attended.

"Good. At least I'll be your first for something," he answered in a satisfied tone before he turned and headed toward his own bedroom.

Ellie sighed. He could have been her first lover; he hadn't wanted that. But he was happy about having her going with him on a party date?

Shaking her head in the dark, she wondered if she'd ever understand exactly how Zane's mind worked. He was a genius, but he was also a man. Did regular men think the way that Zane did?

Somehow, she found it highly unlikely. After listening to years of Chloe talking about her brothers, Ellie knew that Zane was probably unique. Ellie knew she'd never met anyone like him.

As her eyes fluttered closed, she smiled. Somehow, it pleased her more that he'd offered to take her out on a real date than it would have if he'd taken her to bed. Somehow, that was significant, but she was so tired that she fell asleep still wondering exactly what Zane was thinking.

Chapter 9

Ellie couldn't remember a time when she'd felt more out of place. However, she wasn't about to let her nerves spoil her fantasy evening with the most handsome guy at the ball.

She'd had exactly one day to get ready for Zane's charity fundraiser once they'd arrived at his Denver home. Luckily, she didn't find as much organizing that she'd need to do at his place in the city, but there were still piles of paperwork everywhere that needed to be filed and put away.

The Denver mansion was gorgeous. Not that she'd expected it *not* to be, but it wowed her just the same. Unlike his home in Rocky Springs, the bedrooms were all upstairs, making the downstairs living space enormous. Honestly, she wasn't sure she'd even seen every room in the house yet. They'd arrived last night, and she'd been busy most of the day.

Earlier, she'd treated herself to a makeover, getting her hair put up in an elegant style, the short locks almost refusing to be tamed into a sophisticated style. Her makeup had been done by a professional, and she'd chosen a simple cocktail dress in black, a garment that was pricey enough to make her squirm. But she'd bought it anyway, after hanging it back on the department store rack several times because she wasn't sure if she could justify spending that kind of money on a dress. After the dress, she'd needed accessories. All in all, she'd spent more money today than she had in several years in Rocky Springs.

But somehow, she couldn't regret it.

As she'd stood in front of the mirror earlier, Ellie had done a full assessment of herself, and not just the physical body in the reflection. Yeah, she had admitted that she looked nice, but mostly she recognized that she was changing the way she looked at herself. She felt stronger, freer than she'd ever been. Maybe it was her harrowing experience she'd been through, but she had an inkling that Zane was beginning to make her see herself in a whole new way. He liked her. He cared about her. He pointed out things that he really admired or liked about her, and she'd started to take notice of things about herself that she'd never even considered.

She was getting stronger.

She was learning to handle her fears.

She wasn't letting what happened to her shape her life.

She liked what she was doing, and she liked…herself.

Ellie sighed and swiped another glass of champagne from a passing waiter as she made her way back from the restroom, eager to find Zane. She had the most handsome, most intelligent date at the ball, and she wasn't about to let him hang out alone, waiting for her.

He'd made it very clear that she *was* his date, and he'd treated her like a princess. Zane didn't miss the opportunity to tell her how beautiful she looked, and he'd given her a beautiful bouquet of flowers before they left the house because he knew how much she loved them.

Dinner had been amazing. Zane had taken her to a fancy steakhouse, and the food was so good she had a difficult time not moaning with pleasure as she consumed way more than she should have, including the rich dessert.

When they'd arrived in the beautiful ballroom, she had to admit that she'd been intimidated by the blatant wealth all around her, but she'd had Zane there to remind her all of them might be rich, but they were still human, just like anyone else. It had made her relax a little, but everything around her was so perfect and such a stark contrast to her old life that she couldn't help but feel nervous.

Trying to make herself taller by standing on her tiptoes, she scanned the elegant, crowded ballroom for her handsome date. It was pretty difficult to recognize him easily since every man was here in a tuxedo, including Zane.

God, he'd been breathtaking when he'd wandered into the kitchen earlier in the day, perfectly groomed and impeccably put together in his black tux. His face was freshly shaven, his hair still damp from the shower, but he'd looked delicious. Ellie had wondered for a moment if she needed to wipe the drool from her mouth.

She had just finished chugging down her second glass of champagne when she spotted Zane. He was talking to some curvaceous redhead, and he looked uncomfortable. Not that anyone else would notice, but Ellie could see the subtle signs.

Wriggling her way through the crowd, she made her way across the room, hesitating because she didn't want to interrupt him. But when she saw the redheaded female put her finger on Zane's face, tracing the line of his rugged jaw, Ellie saw red, and she was certain he wasn't discussing business.

He's my date, dammit. I feel like Cinderella, and I'm not missing my time at the ball.

Dodging all of the handsomely dressed couples as she steadily made her way to Zane, it wasn't difficult to discern that he wasn't responding at all to the pushy redhead's advances.

Ellie smiled as he grasped the woman's wrist and pulled it from his jaw, his expression stoic as he spoke to her.

Stopping abruptly as she neared the couple, Ellie was momentarily surprised to see that the woman was young, and drop-dead gorgeous.

And Zane was obviously completely and totally…uninterested.

Striding forward, she took her place next to Zane and put her arm on his muscular bicep. "I'm so sorry," she told him with a bright smile that she hoped didn't look as fake as it felt. "The restrooms were busy."

She'd felt him tense beneath her fingers for a brief moment before he realized who was touching him, and then he relaxed as he finally turned his head to look at her. "You're worth the wait," Zane answered smoothly, wrapping a strong arm around her waist.

"Who is this?" the woman who had been fondling Zane asked haughtily.

"My date," Zane answered simply, not even bothering to introduce the two of them.

Ellie spoke up and extended her hand to the gorgeous woman in front of her, refusing to let the female know that she was intimidated. But honestly, she was a little daunted by the flame-haired beauty. "I'm Ellie Winters," she introduced herself simply.

Ignoring Ellie's outstretched hand, the woman glared up at Zane. "You didn't tell me you had a girlfriend," she hissed.

He shrugged and reached for Ellie's outstretched hand and entwined her fingers with his and brought them to his side. "Why would I?" he answered dismissively.

Ellie suddenly saw the woman's expression change from seductive to pouty anger. "I've been trying to get your attention for almost a year, and you pick somebody like *her* over *me*?"

The muscle in Zane's jaw began to twitch, a subtle sign that he was pissed. Ellie had become a master at reading Zane's body language over the last few months since he didn't always express what was on his mind. He might get irritated, but he never lost complete control.

He took a deep breath before he spoke. "I had hoped you'd get the message that I wasn't interested, Elena. Or maybe it's the fact that you're fucking your boss and he appears to care about you that turned me off. Frankly, though, the reasons are irrelevant. You just don't do it for me."

Ellie couldn't help it. She gaped at Zane for an instant before she schooled her expression back to normal. Zane's comment had been spoken in a glacial tone she'd never heard before. As usual, he was blunt, never bothering to explain more than he felt he needed to, but she'd never heard him quite so cold.

Elena? A beautiful name and gorgeous woman who obviously had the heart of a reptile.

The tension in the air was electric as Elena slowly assessed Ellie carefully, and obviously found her lacking. "Do you really think you can compete with me?" Elena huffed.

Ellie forced herself to give the woman a brief, dismissive glance before answering, "There's no competition necessary," she said in a falsely pleasant tone. "I already won." She put a gentle hand on Zane's jaw, and then planted a gentle kiss to the side of his mouth.

Caught off-guard when Zane turned the soft embrace into a possessive kiss, Ellie quickly gripped his shoulders to keep from stumbling in her heels.

Right there, in the middle of a fancy fundraising ball, Zane Colter claimed her, his kiss long and lingering, leaving no doubt that Ellie was exactly what he wanted.

For a moment, her eyes fluttered closed and she let herself drown in the sensual feel of his lips sliding over hers with a pulse of possessive, sultry energy she'd never experienced before.

It wasn't long, and it wasn't entirely sexual, even though it was meant to arouse.

The embrace was more like a covetous demand, and Ellie's heart was skittering, even as he slowly released her mouth.

His gaze clashed with hers, his gray eyes tumultuous and greedy. Her body responded, a deep-seated need for Zane to touch her so acute that she could barely suck in a deep breath.

Finally, Ellie pulled her gaze away, no longer able to see what she knew was reflected in her own hungry stare. "She's gone," she murmured as she stepped back from him.

"I don't care," Zane answered huskily. "Dance with me," he ordered, grasping her hand again and tugging her toward the ballroom floor.

He sheltered her as he plowed his larger body through the crowd, making her a path so she didn't have to dodge around people to follow him. She was breathless by the time she tripped onto the dance floor, tumbling straight into Zane's arms.

"I'm not a very good dancer," she confessed.

"I am. Just follow me," Zane replied as his arms tightened around her and he began moving expertly to the slow melody the orchestra was playing. "Relax," he urged, rubbing one hand gently down her back.

As she began to match his movements automatically, Ellie felt her body melt against him, and she gently laid her head against his shoulder. It became obvious very quickly that he could competently move around the other dancers. "How is it that you dance so well?"

"I'm a Colter. My mom has been involved in charity events as long as I can remember. She taught every one of us when we were young. Most of us try to be at her events out of respect for what she does." He paused for a moment before he added, "Except for her billionaire auctions. Almost all of us managed to bail out of that one."

Ellie laughed softly, loving the feel of his deep voice vibrating against her. "She auctions billionaires?" She had to have misunderstood.

"Yes. If she thinks it will help get her causes out to the general public."

"Tell me." Ellie was curious and wanted to hear the whole story of Aileen's event.

Zane relented, his tone disgusted. "One year, she decided to put billionaires from around the country on the auction block. One night only. One date only. It raised a fortune and got a lot of attention, so now she's trying to do it again."

"Did any of the Colter brothers attend?" Ellie questioned, noticing he hadn't said all of them had gotten out of the event.

"Only Tate. He was still single at the time. The poor bastard. Luckily, he ended up with a winning female who was around eighty years old and just really wanted to talk about her grandkids all night. But he would have been okay with anybody. That's Tate. You know he was always able to charm any female, even in high school."

Zane's voice was thoughtful, so Ellie asked, "Do you think you couldn't have done just as well?" Women were obviously falling all over Zane, albeit not for the right reasons. But somehow she had a suspicion that he didn't feel like he measured up to his brothers.

"I'm a nerd scientist, Ellie. I'm just…different. You know I don't do small talk well, and all of my siblings can charm the hell out of anybody at any kind of party or event. Chloe might not like going to them, but she can play the perfect hostess when she has to."

Leaning back, Ellie looked at the accepting look on Zane's face, and it made her heart swell. "You don't have to be anybody else," she said fiercely. "You're not that nerdy kid anymore, not that there was ever anything wrong with that. You've grown up and matured into the hottest guy I've ever seen. So what if you don't want to talk about the weather unless it's out of the ordinary? Small talk is boring, and you have more important things to discuss."

He raised an eyebrow. "You think I'm hot?"

Zane was teasing, but Ellie was fairly certain there was still a small doubt in his mind about his personal value when compared to his brothers.

Ellie tightened her arms around his neck, the effects of the champagne she'd guzzled making her feel a little bit less inhibited. "I find intelligent men incredibly sexy. You have gorgeous eyes, a hot body, and a mind I admire. You're tenacious, and you're the only person who was still searching for me when everybody else thought I was dead. You're my hero. I would say that puts you pretty high on the fuckable scale for reasons that have nothing to do with your money."

He pressed his mouth against her ear. "I'm not your hero. I'm just a man."

Ellie shivered as his warm breath wafted across her ear, his husky voice making her core clench so hard she missed a step. Zane guided her to a quick recovery before she answered, "An amazing man."

"I don't want you to want me just because I saved your life," he rasped.

Surprised, she replied adamantly. "I don't. I never did. I've always cared about you, way before you saved my life."

The song ended just as she finished her sentence, and Zane dipped her backward, supporting her upper body with his arm as she stretched. Instantly, he pulled her back up again and she slammed up against his rock-hard body.

"You're not wearing a bra," he said irritably.

"How do you know that?" she asked, her words muffled against his chest.

In fact, she *wasn't* wearing much in the way of undergarments at all. The dress had long, off-the-shoulder sleeves, something she hadn't thought about when she'd purchased her ensemble. By the time she discovered she didn't have the appropriate undergarments for the dress, she'd just went without. The material was heavy enough not to show anything, and she wasn't exactly heavily endowed.

"Your nipples are hard. I could tell when the fabric stretched," Zane grumbled.

Everyone was applauding the orchestra and Ellie joined in as she replied, "Then maybe you shouldn't have held me so close and put your sexy mouth against my ear." She turned to leave the dance floor.

Zane caught her arm before she went very far. "Did dancing turn you on?"

Ellie swiped one more glass of champagne from a waiter who was patrolling the edge of the dance floor and took a large sip before she looked up at him. "Not dancing. Dancing with *you* turned me on."

Wordlessly, he took her hand and moved through the bulk of the people until they reached an unused table. He helped her take a seat before he insisted, "Stay here. I'm going to the bar. I think I need a drink."

"They have champagne everywhere," Ellie reminded him.

"I need something stronger than that." He put a hand in one of the pockets of his tuxedo pants, his eyes trailing down the front of her dress. "No dancing with anybody else but me. Do I want to know exactly what you're wearing beneath that dress?"

Ellie downed the rest of her champagne and smiled at him sweetly as she crooked her finger to make him come closer. Giving her a suspicious look, he bent down so she could whisper in his ear. "I've never worn a dress like this, but I didn't want panty lines, so I bought the cutest little black thong with a tiny pink bow, and matching thigh-high stockings. That's it. I feel almost...naked."

Ellie's heart started to pound against her chest wall as Zane turned his head and their gazes clashed and held, his face so close to hers that she wanted to reach out and grasp his hair, make him kiss her until she couldn't think, couldn't breathe.

His eyes were dangerous, a gray so dark and turbulent they reminded her of an incoming thunderstorm. "Jesus Christ, Ellie! Are you trying to be a cock-tease, or are you just being honest?" he whispered hoarsely.

She leaned in closer. "Maybe a little bit of both," she confessed. "I don't flirt. Not usually." She had a feeling the champagne was letting her say exactly what she wanted. When it came to alcohol, she was a lightweight since she rarely even had a small glass of wine.

He put a hand behind her neck, and the intimate, possessive touch made her shiver.

"Don't do it with anyone else but me," Zane demanded, and then placed a rough kiss on her lips before he straightened. "I'll be right back." It sounded more like a warning than a comment.

She watched as Zane strode across the room to the bar, sighing at the tantalizingly sexy male gait of a predator that he used to move from one place to another. Her eyes stayed fixed on his wide shoulders until he finally disappeared into the sea of other dark tuxedos near the bar.

"Ah, here's somebody I haven't met. And you're with Zane. Hello, mystery woman."

A dark-blond male seated himself across from her. His lips were smiling, but for some reason the jovial expression didn't quite reach his dark eyes. "Hello," she answered automatically. "I'm Ellie Winters."

The man reached his hand across the table. "Sean Rycroft," he offered as he shook her hand. "I'm the director of research at Colter Laboratories. Zane's my boss. Well, I suppose he's actually everybody's boss, technically."

"I thought Zane was the director."

Sean laughed. "Hell, no. He's the CEO of the entire global company. He has several directors at all his facilities."

Ellie paused, realizing how little she knew about Zane's industry. "He has labs all over the world?"

Sean nodded. "Pretty much. But most of them are manufacturing facilities to produce the items he's already developed. The main research lab is here in Denver." He paused for a moment before asking, "How long have you two been involved? Zane hasn't said a word. Elena just told me that he had a date."

The redhead? Why had she been talking to this man?

"You know Elena?" Ellie asked cautiously.

"Pretty well, actually. She's my assistant."

So he's the boss Elena was screwing, but now she was looking for an even bigger fish to catch: the owner of the entire company.

Ellie felt sorry for the man sitting across from her. He was probably ten years older than Zane, but he was no troll. He was charming, even if his smile didn't quite reach his eyes; he looked good in a tux, and he seemed nice enough. But how could he *not know* that his viper assistant and girlfriend was searching for more money than Sean apparently made? And Ellie was pretty certain that Zane was paying his directors plenty.

Smiling at him politely, she revealed, "I'm actually Zane's assistant, too. We've known each other for years."

Sean gave her another one of his distant, polite smiles. "Is that right? Fantastic. So you aren't seriously involved? No wonder she's hitting on Zane."

Ellie gaped at Sean, startled by his bluntness. "But aren't you and Elena—"

"She refuses to make a commitment. I think she's still looking for someone better." His voice contained a touch of sadness and bitterness.

Ellie suppressed a shudder of revulsion. Obviously the redheaded snake was using Sean until she found a guy with even more money. The thought was repulsive to her, especially since Sean appeared to care about her.

She accepted another glass of champagne from a passing waiter before she answered. "I guess I don't understand not making a commitment to somebody you're regularly sleeping with." She spoke the comment aloud before she realized she'd done it. Not only did she not understand Elena, but she couldn't contemplate why Sean put up with a woman who gave him so much pain.

Sean shrugged. "Some women are unforgettable. But she wants the high life, and someday I'll get it for her. Right now, at least she's still with me."

"What are you doing, Rycroft?" Zane's angry voice answered from behind Sean.

Sean stood. "Zane," he acknowledged with a nod. "I was just chatting with your new assistant."

"Leave," Zane uttered abruptly. "And don't ever think about spending one second of time alone with Ellie or you'll regret it."

Sean held up his hands innocently. "I thought she was your new assistant."

Zane set his drink on the table, reached out his hand and grasped the lapel of Sean's tuxedo. "Go," he said in a graveled tone. "Right. Fucking. Now." Zane let go and literally pushed Sean away from the table.

Stunned, Ellie stared at the two men as they faced off, Zane's expression so intensely fierce that he looked ready for anything.

She held her breath until Sean finally backed up, turned around and walked away without another word. Able to finally release the air from her lungs, she looked up at Zane, and the look he was giving her was almost frightening.

Had she embarrassed him somehow? Ellie had no idea what the etiquette was for a party like this.

She took a sip of champagne and a deep breath before she gave Zane a questioning look, ready for whatever he had to say.

Chapter 10

Zane wasn't sure what the hell was wrong with him.

One smile. One sweet turn of Ellie's lips in the direction of another guy had been enough to make him completely fucked up.

He sat down and threw back his scotch in one gulp, knowing he was probably scaring the hell out of Ellie. He glanced at her, able to see the confusion on her face.

Pull it together, man. Just because Ellie smiled at another guy is no reason to lose it.

Zane clenched his fists beneath the table, trying to make some sense out of the illogical. Most of the time, he got along fine with Sean. Yeah, he thought he was a fool for messing with a cat like Elena, but that was his business. His director had to know what he was getting himself into. Eventually, he'd need to explain himself to Sean, but he was more worried about Ellie right now.

"Sean does his job, but I don't know him all that well personally. His drama with Elena occasionally gets out of hand, and he's used a few of the female employees to try to make Elena jealous," Zane explained with what he thought was a pretty lame excuse.

"I wasn't encouraging him," she answered calmly. "Is he dangerous?"

Yeah. The conversation had been innocent enough. It had been the only thing that had kept him sane.

Zane shook his head. "I don't know his personal life well enough to know how he treats a woman. I've never had a reason to get into his business. He hasn't been with Colter all that long. All I really know is that he's crazy about Elena, but she's always looking for something better. I have no idea why he puts up with her."

"Zane, I know you want to protect me, but someday I'm going to have to go back into the real world. Someday soon," she told him quietly, her beautiful blue eyes staring him down.

Nope. He didn't like *that* thought at all. Not after all she'd been through. "You are in the real world."

She shook her head. "I've always been alone, solved my own problems."

"Why does it have to be that way again? Why do you have to be alone now when you really need support?" Not that Zane wanted to be just her friend, and it was getting harder and harder each day not to want to be more. Literally *harder*.

She shook her head and broke their locked gazes, her eyes straying to her fluted glass of champagne as she stroked the stem. Hell, even that turned him on. He wanted those caressing fingers all over his fucking body.

Suddenly remembering why he'd been gone so long, he put his hand into his jacket pocket and pulled out the items that he'd bid on and won in the silent auction.

"I won one of the bids on the auctions. I want you to have these." He pushed a white velvet box across the small table.

Truth be told, he'd made damn sure he won by bidding a small fortune on the items. The minute he saw them, he knew they needed to belong to Ellie.

She looked at him in confusion and then down at the box, tracing the decorative gold lettering on the top. "Mia Hamilton?"

He nodded. "She does something special for my corporate fund-raiser every year. The majority of the proceeds this year are going to a joint charity for domestic abuse victims. Mia's sister-in-law founded it. Asha Harrison. They're doing a lot of good work. My brothers and Chloe all support Asha's Fund."

Ellie nodded slowly. "I've heard about it. Lara is involved, too."

"There are a lot of wealthy donors now all over the country. It's a great charity that has very few administrative overheads since they have a lot of volunteers." He nodded at the box. "Open it. I hope you like it."

"Zane, is this a piece by Mia Hamilton?"

"Of course," he answered sensibly.

"I can't believe I'm even touching it. Her stuff is exclusive. I've never seen anything but pictures."

Zane smiled. "Another first," he replied as he impatiently reached over and popped the box open.

Ellie's astonished gasp was audible even in the noisy ballroom.

"Oh. My. God." She leaned back as though she was afraid to touch the jewelry.

Zane hadn't seen all of Mia's work, but he was pretty certain she'd outdone herself on the necklace and earrings she'd made this year. Somehow she'd made a fortune in sapphires, diamonds, and gold still look classy, delicate, and feminine. The chain of the necklace was alternating hearts made of small diamonds and blue sapphires with a slight violet tint. The chain met in the middle to support a heart pendant made of a large sapphire with diamonds framing the center heart. Mia had paired the necklace with simple drop earrings made of the same gems.

"I thought they were pretty. The sapphires almost match your eyes," Zane said anxiously, getting worried about the nervous look on her face.

"Pretty? Zane, these are the most beautiful pieces of jewelry I've ever seen. Can I touch them?"

He reached out and took her hand, placing her fingers on top of the necklace. "They're yours. Of course you can touch them." He was secretly pleased that she seemed so enchanted by Mia's creations.

She carefully traced the delicate hearts on the chain, and then ran a careful finger down the sapphire pendant. "You know I can't accept a gift like this," she told him adamantly. "But I'm really happy that I was able to see these in person. I didn't go to see what was on auction."

He got up and plucked the necklace from the box. Standing behind Ellie, he slipped the chain around her neck and fastened the clasp. He didn't bother with the earrings since Ellie was already wearing a costume pair that he wasn't about to try to take out and replace.

Sitting back down again, he surveyed the stunning contrast of the sparkling gems against Ellie's creamy skin. "Perfect," he declared, satisfied that the necklace had found the place where it had always belonged.

"*Take it off,*" Ellie squeaked, her voice sounding panicked.

He smirked. "Any other time, I'd love to hear those words come out of your mouth, but not this time."

"Zane, I can't wear this. What if somebody tries to steal it? What if the clasp breaks and it gets lost?" She'd leaned across the table so she could speak without attracting attention.

He shrugged. "It's just jewelry."

"Jewelry that costs more than most people's houses," she answered in a frantic tone.

He was getting irritated because her objection was all about how much he spent. Logically, he understood her situation, but he'd never miss a single penny he spent. "It was a gift, Ellie. The money went to a good cause. Christ! Can't you just accept a gift from me without worrying about paying back the money? I want you to have it. It matches your eyes, and sapphires are your birthstone. Coincidentally, they're my birthstone, too."

She lowered her eyes. "I'm sorry. It's such a thoughtful gift, but don't you understand that I'm not used to accepting gifts like this?"

"I do understand. But you have to realize that I'm very used to giving these types of gifts. Not jewelry exactly. But expensive for the average person. For me, it's not that pricey," he reminded her. "It's like you sending flowers to a friend, or buying a card."

Ellie burst into laughter, the sound grabbing and squeezing Zane's heart like a vise. She snorted before she answered, "That really is true, I suppose. But I think I'd be more comfortable with flowers." She fingered the necklace carefully. "And I know it's a good cause. But this is something you need to save for somebody special," she prompted, reaching back to fumble with the clasp of the pendant.

He stood and grasped her wrists. "Don't," he told her gruffly. "I'm ready to go. Are you?"

She nodded. "Yes, but I really need to—"

"Let's get our coats. You can either take the earrings or leave them there for whoever decides to pick them up. I'm not giving them to anyone else. I did give them to someone special. I gave them to you."

He tugged on her wrist to get them to the coat check area.

"Wait!" she answered with panic. "I can't just leave them here, and I need my bag."

Zane released her wrist and let her pick up her small black clutch from one of the chairs, and then observed with satisfaction when she carefully closed the lid of the jewelry box and stowed the earrings safely in her purse.

"You're not playing fair," she snapped at him as she brushed by him.

"You haven't played fair since you decided to wear almost nothing underneath that dress," Zane shot back at her as he clasped their hands together.

"I hardly think that's the same thing," she said tartly, sounding like a sexy schoolteacher.

"Close enough," he replied nonchalantly, continuing to lead her toward the door.

His dick had been hard since the moment he'd seen her in that slinky black dress. Ellie was so naturally beautiful that she didn't need the makeup and hair, but the perfection of how she looked tonight had blown him away. When he'd seen the outline of her pebbled nipples through the black fabric, his cock had started to throb even more insistently.

Mine!

His reaction had been immediate and irrevocable. Ellie belonged with him. Though, he was pretty sure that he needed her more than she needed him.

After she'd revealed exactly what she was wearing underneath that dress, he'd wanted to see if she was teasing him, or if she was telling the truth.

As far as he was concerned, he was done playing fair. Seeing her climax once hadn't been enough. He was addicted. He needed to see her come apart again, hear her scream his name. Oddly, he didn't care if she was a virgin other than the fact that he'd be the first and only guy to claim her, a fact that made him want to fuck her even more. But he hadn't wanted to take her that night because he needed to know that she truly wanted him to be her first. Now, he knew that not only would he be her first…he'd be her one and only.

Honestly, Ellie had always been the one for him. Subconsciously, maybe he'd always known it, but it was pretty damn clear the few times he'd seen her back in Rocky Springs. He didn't act then, which was a fact that he now regretted, but he was going to now.

I almost lost her.

It was pretty damn sad to think that it took Ellie almost dying for him to pull his head out of his ass and find his balls. One thing he knew for sure: he was ready to fight for what he wanted.

No more playing nice. Zane was ready to play dirty, knowing it would be a hell of a lot more satisfying for both of them.

It didn't take long for them to get back to Zane's home. He'd made use of his limo and driver, and they'd been dropped off at the door after a smooth and fast ride home.

The champagne Ellie had consumed was starting to wear off, but she was still riding a little buzz as she asked Zane, "Are you hungry?" They'd stopped into the kitchen to get a drink. She handed him a Coke from the refrigerator, selecting a diet for herself.

When she set the can on the countertop to open it, Zane pinned her from behind, slapping one hand on each side of her. "Not for food. But I'm dying to find out if you've been lying to me all night."

An exploring hand landed on her ass, pinching her butt cheeks and rubbing to see if there was any material underneath. Her breath hitched as he started raising the flowing material up her thighs and to her ass.

"Jesus Christ! You aren't wearing anything else, are you?"

She gripped the counter in front of her and shook her head. "No. I told you I wasn't."

"Turn around," he demanded after he unzipped the back of her dress.

Ellie wanted skin-to-skin contact so badly that she obeyed. "I can't do this," she protested weakly, trying to fight the desires of her body with the logic of her mind. Unfortunately, her body was winning the battle. She'd wanted Zane for so long and so damned much that her defenses were crumbling.

After lifting the dress over her head and letting it hit the floor, Zane took her by the shoulders. "You said you wanted somebody who sees you, somebody who cares about you. I assume you've been saving your virginity for him. That man is me, Ellie. I'm sure as hell not a virgin, but I think I've been waiting for you forever. If you want to back out, do it now, or I'm not sure I'll be able to stop myself later."

His expression was fierce as she glanced up at him, his eyes nearly devouring her mostly-nude body with appreciation.

"I think I've always been waiting for you," she admitted quietly, finally meeting his eyes as they drifted to her face. "But I'm scared."

"Why?" he asked urgently, sounding slightly wounded. "I'd never hurt you, Ell."

She shook her head. "It's not that. I want you. I want to be with you. But after it's over, I'm scared that I'll crave you every single day."

He ran his fingers slowly from the gorgeous necklace that she was wearing down her body until he reached her barely-there panties. His fingers rubbed over the silky material, teasing her with the pleasure she knew she could experience with him and only him. The reason she hadn't had sex before was simple: she'd never wanted anyone except Zane.

"Then crave me, Ellie. For fuck's sake, crave me as much as I crave you," he answered huskily, kissing her forehead, her cheeks, and the side of her mouth. "Need me so badly that you think you're going crazy. I'll be there to take away the ache because I know exactly how it feels."

She felt naked, both emotionally and physically, as she stood before him almost nude. Her arms crept around his neck and she speared a hand through his thick hair, glorying in the feel of the strands sliding between her fingers. "Yes," she answered simply. "Please."

Ellie immediately felt her body being lifted and carried, not knowing where they were going until he set her down in the middle of his own bed. "I want to do this right, Ellie. I don't want you to feel a moment of pain."

She didn't care if it hurt, as long as she could get Zane inside her as quickly as possible. "I don't care. I just want you."

"You already have me," he growled as he started to strip off his clothes. "And I have no intention of letting you go."

She was nervous. Not that Ellie had any desire to back away now. Dammit, she'd almost died at the hands of a sociopath. She wanted to find out what it felt like to be with someone who cared about her, a man she'd wanted for so long she wasn't sure when the deep ache inside her had begun. But her lack of experience was making her anxious.

"I don't know what to do," she confessed, sitting cross-legged on the bed as she watched Zane remove his bow tie and yank it from his neck. Ellie licked her dry lips apprehensively as he started on his shirt, revealing muscular abs and a toned torso that her fingers were itching to touch.

"Anything you want, Ellie. Whatever you need."

"I need to touch you," she said breathlessly as she watched him shrug out of his shirt.

He froze as she slowly scrambled off the bed to stand beside him.

Chapter 11

Following her instincts, Ellie reached down and unbuttoned his trousers, pulling the zipper down carefully. She might have never gone all the way, but she was familiar with the touchy-feely making out part. But it had been a while. She fumbled as she grasped the waistband of his pants and tugged them down, taking the black boxer briefs down with the tuxedo pants.

Dropping to her knees, she kept pulling, surprised when his freed cock almost hit her in the face. "It's enormous," Ellie murmured incredulously as she tried to wrap her fist around his member when it was completely erect.

Zane groaned, and stroked a hand over her hair. "Jesus Christ. I might not live through this."

She let go of him immediately and finished removing his pants and underwear. Zane stepped out of them obligingly. "I'm sorry. Did I do something wrong?" Ellie couldn't hide the worry in her tone.

"No, baby. It's not you." He pulled her to her feet and wrapped his arms around her. "But seeing you on your knees with my dick in your hands is like a goddamn fantasy for me."

Ellie wasn't sure if that was good or bad, but she was totally willing to do it again. "I don't mind fulfilling any of your fantasies," she said eagerly.

He brushed a curl from her face as he replied, "Be careful what you promise, Ell. I have a very dirty imagination when it comes to you," he answered dangerously.

A shiver went up her spine as Zane lowered his hand from her waist to her bare ass, stroking over it as he threaded the fingers of his other hand through her hair. "I need to take this slow, sweetheart. This isn't just a fuck for me."

He picked her up and laid her in the middle of the bed again, but this time he came down on top of her.

"Not for me either," she agreed shakily, the feel of the warm, satiny skin of his chest making contact with her sensitive nipples muddling her brain.

She ran her hands over every inch of bare skin she could touch—over his shoulders, back and then up again—drowning in the sensation of being able to feel him against her skin-to-skin.

"God, you feel so good," she moaned, wrapping her legs around his waist, her body already demanding satisfaction.

"Things are about to feel a hell of a lot better," Zane rasped as he rolled off her body and to her right side.

She mewled with disappointment, hating the loss of connection with him…until she felt his hand cupping her breast, his mouth lowering to suck one of her hard nipples into his mouth.

Ellie had been felt up by guys before, but Zane wasn't just a guy. He was a grown man who knew exactly how to touch her. Squirming as he bit gently on one of the solid peaks, she started to hyperventilate as he pinched the other one.

There was no real pain, and he soothed her with his tongue after the arousing nips and pinches. The combination was so erotic that her core was vibrating with tiny spasms, and she lifted her hips in frustration.

"Zane. Please. I ache."

"I want you to ache," he acknowledged hoarsely as his hand moved down her belly. "I want you to feel, baby. I want you to experience everything."

His fingers brushed over the square of silk over her pussy, making Ellie shudder. "What I want right now is to experience you fucking me," she insisted. She'd waited so long for this moment, and her body was demanding she experience the main event.

"You will," he answered huskily, his words muffled against her breasts. "But not yet." He pulled on her thigh. "Open for me, Ellie. Spread your legs and let me touch you."

His voice was so demanding, so persuasive that she obeyed immediately, spreading her legs apart, feeling so vulnerable that it was almost frightening.

Then, she forgot about her apprehension as Zane traced a finger over the lips of her pussy through the silk, and then promptly gave the panties a hard yank, breaking the strings and causing the garment to come apart in his hand. He tossed the ruined underwear to the floor, after he pulled slow and steady on the thong, letting the soft material slide sensually between the cheeks of her ass.

Totally exposed, Ellie had a hard time not clamping her thighs together, but once he touched her, she was completely lost.

His fingers slid easily through her wet folds, all of them working together as his thumb flicked over her clit while he still caressed the rest of her sensitive pink flesh.

"Oh, God. That feels good. *So* good." Ellie closed her eyes, her back arching as his talented fingers aroused her to the point of insanity. She felt him moving down her body, his hair occasionally brushing her bare skin.

"I hope this feels even better," he answered with a growl.

She squealed as she felt his hot, wet tongue slide over her, zeroing in on the tiny bundle of nerves that was pulsating against his mouth. Zane gave no mercy, devouring her pussy like he hadn't eaten in months. His actions were carnal and raw, his entire face buried between her thighs.

"I can't take it anymore, Zane. Please," she whimpered, her hands sinking into his hair as she felt her impending climax.

Her hips rose up as his fingers found the tight entrance to her sheath and experimentally slipped one finger into her untried body, and then added another. "Baby, you're so damn tight," he cursed, lifting his head for a brief instant while he fucked her with his fingers.

Ellie couldn't reply. Her muscles clamped around his fingers and his tongue brushed over and over her clit; this time, her orgasm rolled over her like huge waves of relief and ecstasy. "Yes. Don't stop. Please don't stop," she begged, her hands urging Zane's mouth harder against her as she gyrated her hips to grind her pussy against him.

The force of her climax stunned her, the strong pulsations rocking her body, not wanting to cease.

Ellie clung to his hair as Zane continued to torment and tease, wringing every drop of pleasure from her that he could get. He licked at the juices she'd released during the powerful orgasm, keeping her in a constant state of arousal.

"Fuck me, Zane. *Please.* I need you," she whimpered, thrashing her head from side to side.

She might have already come hard, but her body wouldn't be satiated until the two of them were joined, locked together with his body pressed against hers. *Inside* her.

"Ellie...sweetheart, I don't have a fucking condom."

His face was suddenly above her, his eyes feral and dark as he looked at her with so much longing that it yanked at Ellie's heart. "I thought all guys carried condoms," she murmured as she wrapped her arms around his neck.

"I don't...I haven't...oh, fuck! It's been a long time for me. Years," Zane rumbled. "I got tired of the bullshit and gave up after I found out my girlfriend was moving on to greener pastures. If I need it, I get myself off."

The thought of Zane stroking himself to orgasm was so erotic that Ellie had to close her eyes on his intense expression. "Fuck me, Zane. I think you already know that I've never been with anyone, and when I went to a follow-up appointment here in Rocky Springs, I asked my doctor to give me birth control."

"Why?" Zane asked in a graveled tone.

"I was on it before I was kidnapped. I had bad periods. But I do it now to make myself feel safer. Don't ask me to explain, because I don't understand it myself. But Dr. Natalie said it's normal to feel afraid of something happening again."

"I know I'm clean," Zane told her bluntly. "But I want you to see the medical documents."

"I don't need papers. I just need *you*," she answered, opening her eyes and feeling the warm rush between her thighs as she met his tortured gaze. "I trust you," she whispered loud enough for him to hear.

Zane stared at her for a moment before he leaned down and kissed her with a longing that her soul immediately answered. She opened to him, let him take her mouth as roughly as he wanted. Ellie wanted to feel his desire, and she kissed him back just as savagely.

He didn't warn her before he pushed his massive cock into her, nor did he hesitate. One stroke and he was deep inside her, and then he stopped, burying himself to the root and pausing so she could get used to his size.

She pulled her mouth from his, panting. "You're so damn big."

Zane let out a groan of pleasure before he replied, "Baby, you're so tight and wet that I'm not going to last very long. Fuck! This all seems so surreal."

Ellie agreed completely. The momentary pain of accepting a cock as big as his was beginning to fade, and her body was insisting he move. Wrapping her legs around his waist instinctively, she swiveled her hips against him, her body begging him to fuck her.

When he started to move, Ellie felt elated. When he started to enter and retreat, pumping into her like his life depended on it, she knew she'd never be the same. The intimacy of their primal connection was physically explosive and blissfully emotional.

Ellie wallowed in Zane's possessive claiming of her body, and she raised her hips to meet every frantic stroke of his cock as their bodies tangled together in one big mass of heat and need.

He reached between their bodies, searching and finding her clit. "Come for me, Ellie. I can't wait any longer. Not this time. But I'm not fucking leaving you behind," he grunted, his finger stroking urgently over her clit as he continued to slam his cock inside her over and over again.

The stimulation on that tiny bundle of nerves forced her to explode, her body feeling like it was being torn to pieces as she started a strong, different kind of climax that she'd never experienced before. *"Yes. Oh, God. It's too much."*

"Let go, baby. Take what you want," he urged desperately.

All she wanted was Zane, and that included seeing him get off. She clung to his sweat-laden shoulder, their bodies sliding together erotically as the pulsations became strong, and then impossibly more intense.

"Zane!" She screamed out his name as sensation overwhelmed her.

He covered her mouth with his, as though he wanted to claim her exclamation of pleasure as his. The kiss was rough, covetous, and greedy, and Ellie welcomed it. She shuddered with ecstasy as the crescendo started to calm, the muscles within the walls of her sheath clamping down on Zane's cock.

Ellie's short nails dug into the skin of his back, needing to find purchase to keep her grounded.

He yanked his mouth from hers. "Fuck!" he groaned, lifting his upper body on his forearms, his head thrown back, every muscle in his body tight as her contractions made him spill himself inside her.

Ellie was panting, her body spent, but her heart was still racing as she watched Zane in his moment of release. He'd never looked more gorgeous than he did right now, his pleasure seemingly so acute that it was almost painful.

Finally, he relaxed, resting his body on top of hers. Ellie gently threaded her fingers into his hair and cradled his head against her shoulder as they both struggled for breath.

"Jesus! Did I hurt you? Please tell me I didn't," Zane said between ragged breaths.

She smiled as she stroked his irresistible head of hair. It was perfect. *He* was perfect. "You didn't hurt me. You were worth waiting for, Zane."

He rose up, causing her fingers to slide out of his hair as he speared her with an intense stare, a look that seemed to be searching to see if she was telling the truth.

Stroking her fingers over the five o'clock shadow on his jaw, she repeated, "You didn't hurt me. Really. My first time was more amazing than I could have dreamed about. Thank you."

"Christ! Don't thank me for something I've desperately wanted for so long. It's not like I was doing you a favor." Zane broke their stare as he rolled onto his back and pulled her on top of him. "It should have been longer and much gentler," he answered in a self-deriding tone as he stroked his hand over her hair and down her back.

She sighed. "It was mind-blowingly amazing." Her spent body was relaxed and still humming with a pleasant post-coital bliss.

"Then you're easily pleased," Zane remarked with a lazy humor in his voice.

"Are you having performance anxiety?" she teased him.

"This was a first for me, too. Maybe a little," he admitted freely. "I can assure you, I've never had any problems before."

Ellie let out a startled laugh at his sudden arrogance. "I'm sure you haven't if what just happened was any indication of your previous performances."

"They never mattered, Ell," he replied hoarsely. "This time, I wanted everything to be good for you."

She had to swallow the lump in her throat before she could speak. "I'm glad it was you," she told him simply, unable to express how much it meant to her that he gave a damn.

All this time, Ellie knew she'd been waiting for this day, this evening. She'd been waiting for Zane Colter, even though he had always been an impossible dream that she just couldn't let go of.

"It will always be me," he grumbled, putting a possessive hand on her ass. "This wasn't a one-timer. I still have all those dirty thoughts about you that I need to make a reality."

Ellie thought for a moment before she spoke. "Zane, I don't want you to feel like you have to do anything more." He'd been hurt by a woman before, and she wasn't going to force their relationship. He bolted into a sitting position, taking her with him. She ended up sprawled over his legs, and struggled into a sitting position right in front of him. He grasped her bare shoulders tightly, his expression troubled. "I do need something, sweetheart," he remarked darkly. "I need *you*. I need both of us to commit to this crazy connection we both know exists. I can't ignore it anymore, Ell, and I don't want you to either. I didn't use a damn condom because I never planned on this being a one-time fling. It's complicated, but I'm past the point where I give a damn. Let's make things as damn confusing as we want them to be. Explore this with me, or I know we'll both regret it for the rest of our lives. At least, I know *I* will."

Her heart skittered as she watched his expression. It went from dark and confused to stubbornly determined. Zane wanted her to be...*his*.

"Monogamous?" she questioned, making sure she understood what he wanted.

He nodded sharply. "For both of us."

She smiled. "I didn't wait this long to toss you away for another guy."

"I don't know what I'd do if you did. I've never felt like this before. Jesus! I'm jealous of any other man who even gets your attention."

"Because of what happened to me?" she queried softly.

He hesitated before answering. "I'm not sure. It's like when you disappeared, I realized that I might have lost something that I should have pursued a long time ago. I've always been attracted to you, but I thought you deserved a hell of a lot more than the mad scientist who knows nothing about a real relationship or romance. And you were Chloe's best friend. Hell, my entire family is almost like family to you. It could have ended up awkward if you weren't interested."

Tears welled up in Ellie's eyes as she watched Zane make himself so vulnerable. *How could he have ever assumed she wouldn't want to go out with him?* "I was infatuated with you when I was in high school, and it never went away, even when you came back to visit when you were in college. But you were so smart, so handsome, and so rich. I told myself that someone like you could never care about a chubby, plain, and desperately poor woman like me. So when you were home, I kept my distance when I could so I didn't make a fool out of myself." Her heart felt like a fist was tightening around it, and her tears flowed faster.

"You were *curvy*, something that got me hard every time I looked at you, sweetheart." He pulled her into his lap and held her like he couldn't let go. "I loved your beautiful blue eyes and crazy sexy blonde hair. You're beautiful, Ell. You always have been. But what I've always liked about you is that you accept me the way that I am. Hell, I'm thinking you even like me the way I am." Zane took a deep breath before he asked, "So can we try this? Can you be happy with a guy who isn't exactly polished with romantic words or one who doesn't always know what to do when you cry like you're doing right now? Oh hell, why *are* you crying?"

She smiled at him through her tears. "Because, even though you profess not to be a romantic guy, I think what you just said was probably the sweetest thing I've ever heard."

Chapter 12

They stayed in Denver for the next few months, and Ellie was happier than she could remember being in her entire life. Most of the day, she worked at her own desk in Zane's enormous office that he never used. Most of his time was spent in the secured research area of the enormous building.

Strange, but she'd never quite realized just how big or multinational his laboratories actually were, or just how much responsibility he took onto his broad shoulders. Occasionally, she had to remind him that he alone wasn't responsible for curing or preventing every health issue in the world.

Lately, he'd smiled and laughed more than she'd imagined possible. She cherished every naughty grin and amused bark of laughter that left his mouth, because she thought he took himself way too seriously.

With ongoing counseling, not only was Ellie starting to recover from her traumatic imprisonment—although there were some things that might never quite go away—but she was also starting to see herself differently. No longer did she look at herself and see a woman who wasn't the least bit interesting or attractive. She saw herself as a woman who was trying to improve herself, be what she should have been before she'd been kidnapped.

With Zane's permission, she'd put a workshop in his finished basement, using the downstairs kitchen that he'd never even touched to set up shop. Slowly, her Internet business was growing, and Ellie was studying and experimenting every chance she got. Her products were beginning to catch on, and suddenly everybody wanted to try some of her aromatherapy fragrances.

Every weekend, she and Zane would go somewhere she'd never been before, and she'd started to actually explore the world outside Rocky Springs and even beyond Denver. Even though she'd always love her beautiful hometown in the mountains, she loved the fact that Zane surprised her with a new destination to see at the end of every week.

Last weekend, he'd flown them to California so she could see the Pacific Ocean, and they'd played like children for two days on the beach.

The nights belonged to them, and Zane had made it his mission to see how many ways he could pleasure her body. Turned out, he really *did* have very dirty fantasies about her, and she had cried out with pleasure through every one of them.

Ellie had reached her goal for weight gain, so she tried to spend as much time getting off her butt as possible. Zane had an indoor pool in his Denver mansion just like he had in Rocky Springs, so she tried to swim every evening, and tried to do some time on the treadmill as often as possible. So far, her weight had stayed steady.

Though, if she were honest, the workout Zane gave her in bed every night was probably why she wasn't gaining weight. He'd taken her to just about every restaurant in the area that he personally liked, every single one of them fantastic.

Her only complaint was that he wouldn't let her settle her old debt with him. He refused to let her pay for anything, nor would he take any part of her paycheck as his assistant to try to pay him back for all that he'd done for her in the past. In fact, he refused to even acknowledge that she owed him anything.

It was the only thing they ever really fought over.

Unlike some couples, the remote control was never an issue. She loved watching the science channels with him, and he'd become almost as addicted to her crime shows as she had always been. They rarely missed an episode of *Supernatural,* but if they did, they were quick to pick it up on demand. It seemed they were equally quirky about what shows and movies they watched.

Tonight, she'd left him watching a documentary on TV to go down to her workshop and pack some products. Ellie made it a point to make sure her orders got out for delivery quickly.

"I missed you," Zane's voice said huskily from behind her.

She'd heard him coming downstairs, but hadn't expected to suddenly feel his hard body pressed against her back. She startled, nearly dropping the candles she was packing.

He stretched out his hand and caught the box expertly, setting it back on the counter.

Ellie's heart still racing, she turned around in his arms. "You scared me," she told him as she wrapped her arms around his neck.

"Totally unintentional," he said remorsefully.

"I know. It's not you. I guess I still have some involuntary reactions that I can't control." Ellie hated it when her rational brain didn't connect with her body sometimes.

Zane took her hand and led her over to the media area with a sectional couch. He dropped onto the middle of it and pulled her into his lap. "Do you want to talk about it?"

No! No, I don't.

Any time it came to really discussing her experiences during her horrific months in captivity, she preferred to pretend it never happened. Natalie never let her get away with avoiding it for long, and some of those sessions were brutally difficult, but Zane hadn't ever pushed her.

She shook her head, but answered, "I don't know. Sometimes I think I'm over it and moving on, but once in a while I still feel the scars inside me that haven't quite healed. I'm not quite sure I'll even have complete closure because he's dead, and he died while I was still in the cabin."

"The bastard took the coward's way out. You never got to see him in court, and you never got to see him pay for what he did," Zane replied angrily.

She nodded. "Exactly. It's like he never existed. It's weird because I was relieved he was dead, but I was angry, too."

"It's not weird, sweetheart. I think it's natural to feel that way."

Ellie sighed, knowing she'd never feel as close to anyone as she did to the man comforting her right now. She didn't want to close him out, and she wouldn't want it from him if he'd gone through something traumatic. "I don't even know where to start."

"Wherever you want," Zane said gently. "Tell me the things that haunt you the most."

"The fact that I didn't get away with his laptop the day it happened. I think about what I could have done differently. Maybe I should have gotten out of the office quicker. Maybe I didn't fight hard enough because I was hoping I could talk him down. Maybe I shouldn't have run, and I could have pretended I didn't know until I had the opportunity to steal his computer from him. There's so many things I could have done differently that might have saved both me and Chloe some pain."

Zane absently stroked his hand over her curls as he answered, "You did the best that you could under the circumstances. Any of those alternatives might have failed."

"Possibly," she agreed. "But I'll never know. There was no opportunity after that to escape. I think I was unconscious during most of the drive to the cabin, so I had no idea where I was. It was disorienting, and he had me chained before my head could clear."

"How often did he come up to the cabin? Did he leave right away?"

Ellie wished he would have left her alone. "No. He stayed that night, using every minute to try to scare me into submission. Every time I argued, he hit me. It was a really long night."

She felt Zane's body tense beneath hers as he asked, "Did he strip you, or did you do that yourself?"

"He used a carving knife to cut off everything I was wearing. A scare tactic, and it worked. I was afraid he was going to rape me, kill me, or both." She took a deep breath before adding, "He took my clothing that first night. When he left the next morning, I was pretty torn up."

"Fuck! I wish I'd suspected him earlier when I could have had him followed. By the time I went back to Rocky Springs convinced it was James, it was too late."

"There's no way you could have known." Ellie stroked his cheek and whiskered jaw. "I'm just lucky you're a genius or I'd be dead."

"Why didn't he leave more supplies? He only left enough for you to barely stay alive."

Ellie shrugged. "I think he wanted me weak and barely living. He also got a kick out of me begging for more food and water. I tried not to, but while I was still semi-alert, I did. I was always thirsty, always hungry."

"He was a sadistic prick," Zane rumbled.

"Very sadistic," Ellie answered sadly. "And when I begged, I gave him exactly what he wanted."

"Don't," he said urgently. "Don't ever blame yourself. Every time he hurt you, it was because he was almost pissing himself with fear because Chloe left him to go work for Gabe. Walker pulled her out of a bad situation."

"Thank God," Ellie replied, sounding relieved. "James never told me that. He just kept saying they were getting married soon. I felt so helpless to do anything to save her."

"You worried about her, and she drove herself crazy trying to find you. I've never seen Chloe as distraught as when you disappeared. I think for a while she was in denial, believing she could find you. When she couldn't, she was destroyed," Zane confided.

"But we're both happy now," Ellie observed wistfully. "I'm not going to let an evil dead man destroy my life or Chloe's."

Zane hugged her tightly and Ellie rested her head on his shoulder. He rocked her tenderly as he said, "I know you won't. Christ! You're the bravest woman I've ever known. And you managed to hold on until I found you."

Ellie smiled against the soft material of his T-shirt. "I think I've spent my whole life waiting for you to find me in one way or another."

"Not anymore," Zane rasped. "Never again. I'll never make you wait for anything again."

"Mmmm…what about last night? I distinctly remember you making me wait." In fact, he'd teased her until she was almost completely crazy with the need to climax.

Zane chuckled. "A different situation altogether. In that particular case, I was going to make it worth the wait. Was it?"

Ellie shivered as she remembered the way her body had come apart when Zane finally stopped teasing her and gave her what she needed. "Worth it, but completely unfair," she admonished him in a faux-petulant voice. "I think it's my turn to make *you* wait."

He pulled her gently back by her hair so he could see her face. "Baby, I'd wait forever if I had to."

The sincerity in his vow sent a wave of tenderness through her heart. He claimed not to be romantic, but his blunt words got to her in ways that nobody else's ever had. She licked her dry lips as she stared into his earnest gray eyes. Every word he spoke was honest, every comment sincere. Her body clamored for her to take this man and savor him for a lifetime.

Zane was special.

And he was hers.

"I have to pack my orders," she said weakly.

"I came down to help you," he retorted. "But I also just got some pictures from Chloe."

Getting on her knees beside him, she started feeling him up for his cell phone. "Let me see," she insisted excitedly, rubbing a hand over the front pockets of his jeans to find his phone.

He stopped her marauding fingers by grabbing her wrist. "Jesus, woman. If you don't stop that you're going to find more than you're looking for," he told her in a husky, warning voice.

"Or I might find exactly what I want," she told him in a sultry voice.

"How fast can we pack those items?" Zane asked desperately.

"Very. But can I see Chloe?" Ellie cherished every picture of her best friend. Occasionally, Chloe sent a video, and she looked so happy. "Where is she?"

Zane fished into his pocket and pulled out his cell phone. "They're in the Bahamas. Their last stop. This weekend we can go home. She'll be back at Gabe's place by then. I'm sorry I couldn't give you more warning. Gabe said they were both getting homesick and were ready to go back to the ranch."

He brought up Chloe's latest text message with a picture. Ellie smiled broadly as she saw her friend with Gabe, a man Ellie only knew very casually. She'd met him a few times, but every time she saw a picture of Gabe with Chloe, she liked him even more. It was clear that Gabe made Chloe happy, and for that alone, Ellie adored him already.

Both of them were smiling at the camera, holding their fancy drinks up as though they were toasting the world. Chloe's lips were turned up in a large, genuine smile that made her eyes glow with joy. Gabe had his arm around her shoulders, grinning like he didn't have a care in the world.

Ellie traced the outline of the couple lightly. "You can tell how much they love each other."

"It's even more obvious in person, believe me," Zane answered, sounding amused.

"I can't believe I'm finally going to see her again. It seems like it's been forever. So much has happened."

"Hey, you're not nervous, are you?" Zane tilted her chin to look at her face.

"A little. I don't want to spoil her happiness now."

"God, Ellie. You won't. Don't you know how damn much she loves you? Seeing you will put the last piece of the puzzle back together again. It will make Chloe complete. She misses you so much, and she's been mourning you even though you're still alive. If anybody is scared, it should be me. She's going to kill me for not telling her the truth. Gabe is probably going to be in trouble, too."

"He knows?" Ellie asked curiously.

"Blake is his best friend. I have no doubt he knows, but he must have decided not to say anything. Chloe pesters me every day about you. I'm glad she's coming home. I hate brushing her off and pretending like I'm accepting the fact that you aren't coming back. Hell, I hate lying to her."

Just the thought of seeing Chloe again after so long made Ellie's eyes moisten with unshed tears. "I'll warn you right now that I'm going to cry, but they'll be happy tears."

"I was pretty sure you would," Zane said unhappily. "But don't do it right now. We have plans," he answered wickedly, plucking his cell from her hand as he stood up and pulled her to her feet.

"Yeah, I need to pack." She turned to go back to her workshop.

Zane snagged her around the waist before she could get very far and picked her up and put her over his shoulder. "I'll do it in the morning."

Ellie found herself hanging upside down in a very undignified position over his shoulder.

"Put me down. You have to climb the stairs," she squealed with both delight and just a little fear of him hurting himself.

He sprinted up the steps effortlessly, ignoring her feeble attempts to pound him on the back to let her loose.

Ellie gave up her struggles as they reached the bedroom, her body already craving his touch.

True to his word, Zane got up early and packed her orders, loading them into the back cargo area of his vehicle so he could drop them off before he went to work.

Ellie wasn't surprised. She'd learned that Zane never uttered anything lightly. For a guy who proclaimed that he wasn't romantic, he was pretty damn thoughtful. For Ellie, the fact that he thought about her needs was pretty heady, and really, Zane's actions were just about the most romantic thing she could ever imagine.

Chapter 13

Spring had come to the Colorado mountains, which really meant that a person never knew whether they were going to need a heavy jacket or shorts.

On this particular day in Rocky Springs, Gabe Walker was dressed in a T-shirt and jeans, his veterinarian wife dressed similarly as she sat on the ground beside him as they watched the water in a small creek that ran through his property trickle along the rocks and continue to move downstream.

"It's so good to be back," Chloe said wistfully. "Traveling was amazing, but I missed my family and our home."

Gabe was pretty sure she missed the horses a lot, too, but he didn't mention it. He had too much on his mind, and he was terrified of putting a wall between him and the woman he loved more than anything or anyone else in the world.

Chloe had healed from most of the emotional pain James had put her through, but her wounds had been deep, and the last thing Gabe wanted was to tear any of them open again.

Maybe I should have told her.

It wasn't like he hadn't considered it, but for several reasons, he hadn't. He'd broken the news that James had committed suicide a while ago, knowing she was strong enough to handle it. But he hadn't shared the one other thing that he knew meant everything to Chloe: that her best friend was alive and recovering.

"Chloe, I have something to tell you, and I hope you'll hear me out," he started haltingly.

She turned her head and looked at him, her expression concerned. "Is everything okay with you?"

"It's fine. Really fine. But I have some news."

He watched as her worried expression grew bleak. "About Ellie?"

Gabe swallowed hard and nodded.

"Did they find her body?"

The sorrow in his wife's voice nearly broke him. "Yes and no." Holy hell, he couldn't keep making things worse. He needed to just spit out the truth and stop making his wife anxious. "Chloe, she's alive. Zane found her."

"Oh, my God! Is she okay? Where is she?" Chloe jumped off the ground like her ass was on fire. "I have to see her, Gabe."

He grabbed her shoulders to keep her from running back to her mare and galloping away to find her friend. They'd ridden to this spot and he'd deliberately stopped here to take a break so he could be completely alone with her to break his news.

"Listen to me, sweetheart. She's fine. She's with Zane, and they won't be here until this afternoon. They're flying in from Denver."

Chloe frowned at Gabe. "Where has she been all this time?"

It was one of the hardest questions Gabe had ever had to answer. "She was kidnapped by James and held prisoner in a remote hunting cabin. Chloe, she was in pretty bad shape when Zane found her. If he'd found her any later, I'm afraid she wouldn't have made it."

"But James has been dead for months," Chloe muttered irritably.

"Zane found her soon after we left," Gabe confessed.

Her expression filled with hurt. "He never told me. In fact, he pretty much lied."

"I know. We all did. Blake told me after she was found, but I knew you needed time to heal. Besides, Ellie didn't want you to know."

"Why?" Chloe asked tearfully. "She's my best friend."

He nodded. "That's why she didn't want you to know. She was in pretty bad shape, and she didn't want you to blame yourself for what happened to her."

Chloe shrugged Gabe's hands off her. "That's the way Ellie is—concerned about everyone except herself. But you all knew. Anybody else could have said something. God, she needed me. After that many months gone, she must have needed help."

"Zane took care of her, Chloe. She didn't need anything."

"It doesn't matter. I should have been told. God, you let me keep believing she was dead! How could you? Do you know how badly I was mourning her loss?"

"I knew. But I didn't want you to blame yourself either."

Chloe turned her back to him and leaned against a nearby tree. "Of course I blame myself. I got her the job with James. I led her right into his big fat web of evil." She took a deep breath before adding more calmly, "Tell me the whole story."

As he stared at his wife's back, Gabe explained as much as he knew about what had happened to Ellie. He knew Chloe was listening intently, but she didn't speak.

When he'd finally spilled every detail that he knew, she turned to face him, her expression filled with betrayal and hurt. "So you all decided that poor little Chloe wasn't strong enough to deal with the truth."

"We all thought it best to not stress you, sweetheart, yes."

"What did you think was going to happen? Did you think I'd crumble? I wouldn't have. I would have been happy, dammit."

"We knew that. But you'd been through hell. I didn't want you eating yourself up over Ellie's condition. She didn't want that either."

"You're my husband, Gabe. I trust you more than any other person on Earth."

"Don't you think I know that? Do you think it was easy for me to keep this to myself? Yes, I did it so you could have some time to heal, but I also did it because Ellie wanted it this way. She didn't want you to rush back to Rocky Springs to take care of her when you had your own wounds to heal."

Chloe ran her hand over her face, her expression horrified. "Oh, God. She saw those horrible videos."

"It doesn't matter. She's your best friend, and she realized you didn't know they existed." Only a few people had seen Chloe's videos, and Gabe had been one of those people. He shook off the anger he harbored for a dead man that swamped him all over again, trying to focus solely on Chloe.

"All of this happened to her because she was trying to help me. How do I live with that? And how do I forgive all of you for not telling me that she was alive?" Chloe's voice was tearful and desperate.

Gabe moved forward, but Chloe shied away from him, and that hurt him more than anything else ever could. "You'll have to forgive me, sweetheart. And you'll have to forgive your family. We all knew you were strong enough to handle the truth, but you were still trying to work things out. *You* needed to be your priority—and I won't apologize for putting your needs first. Ever. You needed to leave Rocky Springs, just like Ellie needed to get away from here for a while." His heart was hammering against his chest wall as he added, "I'm not me without you, Chloe. You have to forgive me because I can't be without you anymore."

"I hate it that I can't hate you," she told him angrily.

Gabe wanted to laugh at her comment, but he didn't dare. "Face it, darlin'—if you had to make the same call, you'd do exactly what I did. You'd think about protecting me if I was vulnerable."

She stared at him for a moment thoughtfully. "I honestly don't know what I'd do. But I know it would kill me to lie to you."

"Technically, I didn't lie. I just didn't tell you the truth." It was a lame argument, but he was desperate enough to try anything.

Chloe put her hands on her hips and gave him an irritated glare. "In this case, I don't think there's much difference."

Gabe released a frustrated breath. "I didn't want to do it, Chloe. But if I had to do it again, I would. Yes, I was protecting you. I love you more than anything or anybody else in this world. There isn't much I wouldn't do to see you as happy as you've been for the last several months."

A tear trickled down Chloe's cheek, and that tiny droplet was all it took to break Gabe's heart.

"I can't believe she's alive," Chloe said hesitantly, her tears starting to fall faster.

Gabe felt his phone vibrate and he pulled it out of his pocket. "She's not only alive, but she's back here in Rocky Springs. Zane said they just landed and are headed for his house."

Chloe started to cry in earnest, painful sobs pouring forward from deep inside her.

Gabe opened his arms, holding his breath as she hesitated infinitesimally, and then she ran forward and flung herself at him. He caught her up and cradled her against his body, knowing she'd forgiven him and everything was going to be okay. As he held her tightly against him, knowing she was everything to him, he vowed to himself that no matter how difficult it might be, he'd never ever risk losing her again. He was an open book to Chloe. She knew him, and she knew all of his secrets. From this day forward, now that she was stronger, Gabe swore he'd never keep anything from her again.

Zane was apprehensive as he pulled into the garage of his home at Rocky Springs. Gabe already knew they were here, and he had no doubt he'd be seeing his little sister and her husband in the next few hours. Gabe had let him know he and Chloe were headed back to the house to shower, and they'd set a time to meet in the early evening.

Hell, he'd already been warned that Ellie was going to cry, and for whatever the reason, he didn't like to see her torn up. Okay. Yeah. Maybe they'd be happy tears, but Ellie and Chloe were bound to dredge up some of their pain while they worked through all that had happened.

He took a deep breath as he cut the engine on the vehicle and closed the garage door. It had been a weird day. First, Elena had come up missing. Sean had called him, accusing Zane of somehow being responsible for her absence. The rant hadn't made a lot of sense, but Zane brushed it off since he knew how attached to Elena his director was, even though she didn't deserve it.

Zane had tried to explain that more likely than not, Elena would be back, but Sean hadn't been in the mood to listen. Honestly, the guy had sounded distraught.

More than likely, she'd found a richer man than Sean.

Zane paid very well for a man in Sean's position. Unfortunately, he knew that his director had lavished Elena with luxuries, some that were incredibly costly. Keeping up with the demands of a woman like her had to eventually leave the poor guy broke.

Trying to push his strange conversation with Sean from his mind, Zane smiled at Ellie as she met him at the door.

She shot back a tentative smile.

She's nervous.

Zane unlocked the door, and then he led the way inside.

He looked around the immaculate kitchen and then peeked into the living room.

"Oh, my God. The house looks amazing. What did you do?" Ellie asked, her tone slightly awed.

Ellie had gotten a lot of things organized before she'd left this house, but it hadn't been this clean and not nearly as inviting. Zane had a feeling Ellie hadn't wanted to intrude, or put anything of herself into either of his homes, so he'd done it himself.

As requested, there were various fresh flower arrangements around the home, something that Zane had specifically requested for Ellie's homecoming. Her work supplies for her aromatherapy had been duplicated, the new stuff stowed neatly in the pantry. There wasn't a speck of lint or dust on the floor, and the decorator he'd hired had changed the downstairs space to something lighter and brighter. It was a contemporary look that would suit Ellie, so much different than the previous traditional, heavy décor.

Honestly, Zane preferred the change himself. When he'd built the house, he hadn't really given any input into what kind of feel he wanted inside the house. He was more interested in the design and getting all of the rooms and amenities he wanted. He'd told the initial decorator to make things functional, and she'd done exactly that. The woman had used expensive, heavy furniture and ornate designs that she probably assumed a wealthy man would want.

"Oh, my God. What *did* you do?" Ellie repeated in amazement as she twirled around, as though she was trying to take in her new surroundings.

Zane watched as she peeked into the family room, her eyes growing wide. "My pictures are in here," she said with confusion. "And some of my old throw pillows."

Zane already knew that. He'd asked the decorator to incorporate any of Ellie's items from her old place that she could before the rest were stored. Obviously, she'd found some things that worked.

Since Ellie hadn't budged from the doorway of the family room, Zane went and took her hand, leading her past the kitchen and into the living room. "What do you think?"

She opened her mouth, and then closed it again as her eyes lit on a collection of photos over the couch. "That's us," she said in a hushed tone, walking over to the pictures and staring.

Zane let her tug him along with her, and he nodded at the wall, happy to see how well the wall collection had come out. Every image was framed beautifully, arranged in a pattern that looked natural.

"I know," he finally answered. "I collected all of the pictures I took wherever we went and asked them to be finished out on the wall."

She finally turned to him, her expression perplexed. "Why?"

He shrugged. "Because you were always so worried that you didn't have a real home. I wanted my houses to be your homes, too. Our homes. I wanted to see our things mingled together, to know that it wasn't just me living here. We live here together." He took a deep breath before asking a question he dreaded. "You don't like it?"

"I love it," she replied in a tremulous voice. "It just makes us really…entwined here."

That was exactly what Zane wanted. He wanted the two of them to mesh so tightly that Ellie would never want to leave. "I know. I like it that way. I told you this wasn't a quick fling for me, Ellie. I want you to stay in our homes. I want to smell your scent lingering everywhere. I want to see your things next to mine. Fucking hell, I want to tie you to our bed so you can never leave."

She turned to look at him, her bright blue eyes sparkling, wet with tears. "I want that, too. I just can't believe you did all of this for me."

"It was partly for me, too," he admitted. "I'm a selfish, greedy bastard who wants to make sure you have every reason to consider this as much your home as mine. I want you to stay."

With an emotional sob, Ellie threw herself at him, and Zane happily caught her.

"I can't believe you're concerned for a single minute that I'd go anywhere," she told him, sounding astonished. "Tie me to your bed. I'd happily stay there."

"I wasn't kidding," Zane told her huskily. "But I'd never literally restrain you, Ellie. Not after what you've been through."

Christ! He actually had dirty fantasies of having Ellie exactly where he wanted her, but it was one fantasy he'd never act out. His damn primitive caveman instincts to conquer and keep her would have to go screw themselves.

Sexually, Ellie was open to trying just about everything. In fact, she had an earthy lust for him that drove him insane. And the woman was an adventuress when it came to trying out new ways to drive each other crazy in the bedroom. But bondage was one thing he refused to do.

"Zane," she whispered against his ear. "I trust you. If the thought turns you on, it will turn me on, too. I guarantee it."

"No," he answered simply, grasping her tightly around the waist and glaring at her stubbornly.

She gave him a sultry smile. "I thought you like acting out your dirty fantasies."

"I do. But not that one." He heaved a masculine sigh. "Stop looking at me like that."

"Like what?" she asked innocently.

Damn! She was far from innocent now that he'd been unable to keep his hands off her since the first time he'd taken her. That heated, carnal look worked on him every time.

Chapter 14

Ellie clasped his hand and led him determinedly to his bedroom.
What Zane had done to make her feel like his home was also
hers had touched her in a way she'd never experienced before.
She refused to be a woman with hang-ups anymore. Anything he'd
ever done to her sexually had been orgasmic. There was no reason
for him to believe she wouldn't play with him just because she'd been
held prisoner by a monster.

This was Zane.

This was a man who cared about her.

This was the man…she loved.

There! She'd admitted it. She loved him. Ellie couldn't say exactly
when her fondness and infatuation that she'd had as a teenager had
morphed into a love that rocked her to her soul. But she was pretty
sure it hadn't taken long. Her trust in him was complete, her love
endless. Now, she wanted to prove it by giving him total control of
her body and her heart.

If she couldn't seem to confess how she felt in words, she was
going to *show* him.

"Ellie, I don't care how hot it might be, I can't do it," Zane growled
as he stopped beside her in the bedroom.

"Why?" She grabbed the hem of the lightweight shirt she was wearing and pulled it over her head.

The bra went next as Zane stayed mute, but she could see his eyes caressing her. She shucked off her jeans and panties, not the least bit shy as she stood before him completely nude. She'd lost her shyness with him weeks ago. He knew exactly what her body looked like. Every scar. Every imperfection. And he appeared to love it exactly the way it was.

Nonchalantly, she sashayed to the closet and pulled out a cream and navy-blue tie she'd never seen him wear, and then took it to him and held it out. "Do it. You know you want to." Zane liked to be in control, and she had no problem giving it to him. It was glorious to watch him the moment he snapped.

She climbed on the bed and raised her arms, clasping two of the wooden posts on the headboard.

"Ellie," he said dangerously, starting to slowly and methodically remove his clothing, but she could tell he was rattled.

"I'm never going to be afraid of anything you do to me." In fact, her body was already clamoring for her to touch him as he revealed his powerful body slowly.

Her eyes wandered from his muscular chest to one very aroused cock as he kicked his jeans and boxer briefs aside, leaving him completely naked.

His eyes had never left her provocative position, his expression growing darker and darker as he climbed onto the bed. He'd tossed the tie beside her, but he picked it up again as he moved toward her.

"You're aroused," she purred.

"Jesus, Ell! With you, it doesn't take much. All I have to do is think about you and I'm cocked and ready to fire," he told her angrily. "I don't need to tie you to my bed."

"I wish you would," she said encouragingly. "I've known what it's like to be confined by an asshole. I'd much rather make a better memory."

His expression was unreadable as he seemed to think about her words. He met her eyes, and they stared at each other, Ellie trying to silently communicate her feelings.

Suddenly, he straddled her body and quickly took the tie and knotted her hands together, and then connected the ends to the headboard. "One look of fear, one flinch, and I'm letting you go," he said hoarsely, his eyes moving hungrily over her face, and then he secured her hands above her head.

"I'm not scared, Zane. I'm turned on." There was something freeing in the fact that she didn't have to make any decisions right now. She was at Zane's mercy, and she wanted him to satisfy her now.

He leaned down, supporting himself with his hands, as he whispered huskily in her ear, "You'll be even hornier shortly," he warned.

"No teasing," she begged.

He lowered his head and kissed her, stopping her from getting out any more words. His dominant embrace fueled the fire that was already smoldering, just like setting fire to gasoline.

She pulled on her wrist, automatically wanting to twine her arms around his neck.

When he broke the embrace to move his tongue down her neck and to her breasts, Ellie was already half crazy. "Please," she pleaded. "Fuck me."

He lifted his mouth from her skin long enough to confess, "I love it when you talk dirty to me. I love it when you're so desperate that all you can think about is me inside you."

"I'm more than desperate," she whined, wrapping her fingers around the taut restraints and clenching them so hard that the fabric would never be the same.

He nipped and tongued her breasts, alternating from one to the other, and Ellie squirmed beneath his touch, needing to feel all of him.

Shivering as he moved his mouth down her belly, she raised her hips, unable to voice her need.

Just when she was ready to scream with frustration, Zane moved back, shoved her legs apart and moved between them. "Tell me you want me, Ellie. Say it," he demanded.

His mouth was so close to her pussy that she could feel his warm breath on her core.

"I need you. Please, Zane."

"What do you need?"

"I need you to make me come. Now," she insisted, desperate to do so, but unable to grasp his hair and shove his head between her legs.

She quivered as she finally felt the light touch of his mouth on her, his tongue gently delving between her folds. Pushing her legs up and back, he licked her from anus to clit, lapping up everything he could get before his tongue flicked over the tiny bundle of nerves that was pulsating as her core clenched almost painfully.

His mouth devoured her, his tongue tortuously exploring her pussy. She moaned as the pressure on her clit became harder and harder. "Yes. Yes, please. *More*," she pleaded desperately in a voice she hardly recognized as her own.

Just as she was ready to orgasm, he pushed her over the top, thrusting two fingers into her channel and filling her, thrusting in and out furiously, matching the crazy rhythm of his tongue.

Her gut twisted, and then the pleasure flowed through her entire body, centering on the ferocious, carnal pleasure she was getting from relying on Zane for every wave of erotic pulsation that was overwhelming her body.

Ellie's climax crashed over her body explosively, uncontrollably. "Zane!" She screamed out his name as her fists clenched the ties that bound her to the bed.

He prolonged her ecstasy as long as he possibly could, never slowing down his endless pursuit to lap every ounce of her juices like a man who hadn't had anything to drink for days.

Ellie's thighs and pussy were still quivering as Zane reared up, his eyes instantly meeting hers. "Jesus, Ellie! You look so damn…" He looked as if he was searching for the words. "*Mine*," he concluded fiercely.

She panted, trying to catch her breath. "Then take what's yours," she gasped, desperate for him to be inside her. "Please."

His face registered a feral, possessive expression before he reached up, released her hands from the bindings, and then flipped her onto her belly, urging her up on her hands and knees. Surprised, Ellie did what he wanted, knowing he wanted to claim her in the most primitive way possible. He'd never done this before, generally preferring they were face-to-face when he was fucking her into a state of madness, wanting to see her come.

The slap to her ass was firm and she jolted in shock as he grunted. "Never push me this far, Ellie, or this is what you'll get." He smacked her rear a few more times, and then rubbed his hand covetously over the stinging flesh. He delved between her thighs, stroking her pussy after every erotic smack.

She moaned as he finally entered her from behind, burying his cock to the root. The sensation was so damn erotic that she couldn't stop groaning with pleasure, her hands clenching the sheets beneath her.

Gripping her hips, Zane showed her no mercy as he pummeled her over and over again with his cock, pulling her ass back against him with every thrust.

"Oh, my God, Zane! Yes!" He felt so deep in this position, and she knew he was as lost to this carnal mating as she was right now.

Ellie could feel her body perspiring, feeling like she was burning from the inside and it was spreading outward to every inch of her flesh. Pushing back, she tried to make their bodies meet harder, the slapping of their flesh and harsh breathing the only sounds in the room.

"Harder," she urged, not wanting him to stop.

"Good," Zane rasped. "You feel so fucking good."

"Yes," Ellie hissed, pushing back as he pulled on her hips, needing him so desperately that only this rough, hard mating was going to satisfy her.

"Tell me you're *mine*, Ellie. Tell me that you'll never leave," he rumbled, tightening his hold on her flesh as he pounded into her.

That was exactly what she'd been trying to show him. In his desire to comfort her, help her through her pain, he'd been suffering through his own discomfort alone. "I'm not going anywhere. I'm not leaving you again," she answered breathlessly, trying to take away the fear that was the most acute for him.

He's afraid. He's worried that I'll disappear again.

It wasn't a rational fear, but Ellie had learned that very few things that she was still anxious about made sense.

She imploded the moment she felt Zane's fingers stroking over her pussy and then over her clit, his hand having moved from her hip to the pulsating nub.

Zane took over as Ellie's climax consumed her. "Come for me, Ellie. I can't wait any longer," Zane insisted in a graveled voice.

He didn't need to tell her to lose it. The muscular walls of her sheath were already clamping around his cock in spasms she couldn't control, signaling to Zane that she was already climaxing...hard.

"Christ! There's no better feeling than you coming around me," Zane groaned.

Ellie dropped to her elbows, unable to keep herself supported on her hands as her orgasm peaked and Zane spilled himself deep inside her with a tormented groan.

Lowering himself over her, Zane kissed the back of her head and both sides of her face, and then rested his forehead against her hair.

She could hear and feel his labored breathing, the warmth of his rapid exhales ruffling her hair, his chest rising and falling against her back.

Ellie finally collapsed completely, and Zane rolled to her side.

When she could finally get the words out, she whispered, "I'm hot."

"Already?" Zane teased as he played with a lock of her hair.

She slapped his arm playfully. "You know what I mean. I'm sweating like a pig."

"Me, too," he agreed as he rolled to his feet at the side of the bed. "Let's go."

She shook her head. "You wore me out. I need a few minutes."

He didn't say a word as he bodily picked her up and made his way out of the bedroom and to the indoor pool. He lowered them both into the water slowly, cradling her nude body against him, submerging them slowly so it wasn't a shock to her system.

As she lowered her feet lazily to the tiled floor of the pool, Zane took her wrists gently and turned them over and back again, inspecting the flesh. "Thank God. No marks," he mumbled, and then put a gentle hand on her butt, stroking over it tenderly. "But your ass is a little red." He didn't sound particularly remorseful that he'd left some kind of brand on her.

Wrapping her arms around his neck, she teased, "It was worth it. I don't think I've ever come quite that hard."

A relieved grin lit his face. "I didn't want to hurt you, Ell. Thank you for trusting me that much."

"You'd never intentionally hurt me." She stroked a hand over his shadowed jaw. "I know that."

"I don't want to do it unintentionally either," he grumbled, tightening his arms around her waist, and then lowering his head to kiss her.

Unlike their wild session in bed, his kiss was tender and sweet, an affirmation of how much he wanted to cherish her. Ellie's heart melted as his lips gently roved over her mouth, licking and tasting every inch.

When he finally lifted his head, she sighed and laid her head on his shoulder, the water lapping around them, steadily cooling her body down. "The house looks amazing. Thank you," she whispered huskily into his ear.

His gesture had touched her more than she could explain.

"Our house," he corrected. "I want it to feel like home to you."

"It does." Ellie was starting to feel like anyplace was home for her as long as Zane was there with her.

"Good." He nodded. "I think it finally feels like home to me, too."

Stepping back, she dunked her head to completely cool herself off. She surfaced, pushing her wet hair from her eyes as she reminded him, "It's always been your house."

Zane followed suit, plunging beneath the water before answering. "Maybe. But it was never a home. Maybe that's why I never gave a damn how it looked. It was a place to sleep, a place to stay, a place to be near my family. But it was just a house then."

Ellie's heart pounded wildly. "But now it feels like a home to you?"

"It is with you here. It feels like us."

His comment was so endearing that she hugged him, and then clung to him, wrapping her legs around his waist. She savored that moment of intimacy as Zane hugged her to him, both of them bonded tightly together.

Finally, when she opened her eyes, Ellie's gaze caught the clock on the wall of the pool area. "Oh, shit! It's almost five o'clock. Chloe and Gabe will be here soon."

Gabe had texted Zane that they'd be over around six o'clock, but her friend had a habit of arriving early.

"Hey, don't worry," Zane said with some humor in his tone. "Just tell her you got tied up."

Ellie smacked his arm playfully. "That's not funny. Oh, my God. She'll know. Chloe always knows when I'm lying. She says I'm a terrible liar."

Zane laughed. "Then don't lie. You *were* tied up. You don't have to tell her that her brother was fucking you like his life depended on it, which it did by the way. I think I would have expired from a case of blue balls if I couldn't get inside you."

"Oh, God," Ellie groaned loudly. "I'm not sure she'll like the fact that I'm doing her brother."

"It's none of her business," Zane replied more seriously. "And I don't plan on stopping. So I guess she'll have to get used to it."

"It might be…awkward," Ellie warned him.

He shook his head. "No, it won't."

"I need to take a shower and get ready," she said anxiously as she disentangled her body from his and started back toward the steps.

He followed her, grabbing a towel to dry her off, and then swiped it over his own body before handing it back to her as she held out her hand. He gave it to Ellie, and she quickly dried off her hair.

Zane gestured toward the door. "Stop worrying, sweetheart. I can see that worried expression on your face. Chloe just wants to see you again. Let's go take a shower."

"I'm not showering with you," she said sternly. Ellie knew exactly what would happen if she stepped into the shower with Zane. They couldn't be naked together without wanting to touch each other.

"We are," he said nonchalantly. "There's no way I'll give up the chance to spend any time with you naked."

Ellie was secretly delighted, but she threw her towel at him. It landed squarely on his head. "Pervert," she accused.

"That's your fault." He put the blame on her with a sexy grin as he leered at her breasts.

She giggled like a young girl, surprising herself at how much she enjoyed his sexually playful side. Tossing the towel, she sprinted for the master suite bathroom. "I'll lock the door."

He followed, hot on her trail. "Bullshit!"

He chased her naked through the house. She made it to the shower, but didn't have time to close the door before Zane caught up to her.

Ellie never admitted it was a half-hearted attempt. She'd *wanted* him to catch her, and he did. However, she was hard-pressed to make herself presentable by six o'clock.

Chapter 15

Blake Colter was just getting ready to get into his pickup truck when he saw Marcus's Ferrari 458 Spider cruising down his driveway.

"Shit!" he cursed, wondering if Marcus was slumming it today since he wasn't driving one of his most expensive vehicles. His twin appreciated doing everything fast: fast cars, fast planes—and fast women, because he never stayed with one for very long.

Blake wouldn't categorize Marcus as a rich snob. Granted, the guy liked the finer things, and Marcus liked to get to where he was going a lot faster than everybody else. In some ways, he understood why Marcus had a need for speed since he secretly worked for the CIA during his constant travels all over the world to manage the Colters' global interests. But Blake worried about him. Some of the shit he got himself into wasn't wise if he wanted to stay alive during his business trips.

Hesitating with the door of his pickup truck open, Blake waited for Marcus to smoothly step out of the low-slung vehicle and saunter up to him.

"Where are you going?" Marcus questioned curiously as he stopped beside Blake.

"I thought I'd swing by Zane's place. I'd like to see Chloe and Gabe."

Marcus lifted an arrogant brow. "Already? They just got back. Chloe and Ellie are just meeting for the first time since Ellie disappeared." He hesitated before adding, "You just want to spy on the reunion."

Blake squirmed. What Marcus was saying was partly true. He *did* want to see how things were going when Ellie and Chloe saw each other for the first time in months. Chloe had presumed that her best friend was dead, so it wasn't going to be an easy or quiet reunion. "Yeah? So? Maybe I do want to see them together. They've both gone through hell. Other than Chloe marrying Gabe, it's the only good thing that's happened to either one of them." He knew he sounded defensive, but he didn't give a damn.

"What about Zane and Ellie?" Marcus questioned.

"What about them?"

"I think Zane's going to end up being the next Colter to get hitched."

"You think they've gotten that close?" Blake thought Zane liked Ellie, but he didn't think it was serious. His younger brother had always been the type to step in when somebody needed him. Underneath Zane's brilliant mind lay a tender heart.

"I think they're very…close," Marcus answered, sounding amused.

Blake brushed off Marcus's comment. If things were serious between Ellie and Zane, everybody would know. "Did you come over for something specific?" he asked.

Marcus motioned for him to get in the truck. "You drive. But be careful backing up. I don't want you to hit my car."

Blake watched as Marcus walked casually to the other side of the truck and got in. Hopping into the driver's seat, he glared at him suspiciously. "You were always planning on going, too. That's why you came over."

Marcus shrugged. "Maybe," he said noncommittally.

Blake was tempted to back his heavy truck into the sports car behind him just to get a reaction. Lately, Marcus had grown cooler and more distant. Maybe it was because of the work he did for the government. It had been gradual, but Blake could sense things with Marcus. The two of them had always been able to read the other's emotions. Sadly, Blake was starting to comprehend less and less from Marcus. It was as though he'd put up a shield to keep everybody from knowing what he was thinking.

"Do you remember when I did you that favor, pretending to be you so you didn't have to go to a party?" Marcus asked carefully.

"What party?" They hadn't done a switch since they were teenagers.

"The one you dreaded because you said the female host was as bossy as a drill sergeant."

Blake turned and looked at Marcus in surprise. "We were eight years old, Marcus, and I said she reminded me of Cruella De Vil, which definitely fit her perfectly."

Although the incident had happened a long time ago, Blake could still remember how disappointed he'd been because Cruella's sister wasn't attending the birthday party. And the last thing he wanted was to attend the party without Cruella's sibling as a buffer.

"I don't know. I kind of liked the little drill sergeant," Marcus mused. "Anyway, you said back then if you could repay me some day by doing the same thing, you would. You still up for that?"

"You want me to be you? We're in our mid-thirties. And you're asking for a favor I promised when we were eight? Hell, I pretty much forgot the whole thing."

"I never forget. And I don't need it right now," Marcus reassured him. "But possibly in the future."

"What are you up to, Marcus?" Blake would swear there was more to this question and answer session than he knew.

"I can't tell you that right now," Marcus remarked with a hint of remorse in his tone. "As long as you're a senator, my personal activities are off-limits to sharing."

"I already know what you do for the CIA," Blake reminded him as he turned the corner and headed toward Zane's house.

"It's not about them," Marcus answered thoughtfully. "Not directly anyway."

"Then what?" Blake was getting antsy. He wanted to know what in the hell Marcus was cooking up this time.

"I'll tell you some day. I'll tell all the family. But trust me, I can't right now. I just need to know you'll help me if I need it."

"Of course I'd help you. It goes without saying. You're my brother." Blake was irritated that Marcus wouldn't share more, but he'd certainly be there if his twin needed him.

"Good."

Blake knew the one-word answer was all he was going to get. "When might this happen?"

"I don't know if I'll *ever* need that favor. But it always pays to know all of my options."

"Just keep your ass safe, and you won't need anything," Blake told him gruffly.

"I plan on it," Marcus answered arrogantly.

Blake had no answer for that comment. He wanted all of his family to stay safe, and he wanted them all happy and secure.

They drove the short distance in silence, Blake lost in thought about why in the hell Marcus would ever need him to play a game of switch.

"Going somewhere?" Tate Colter asked his wife innocently.

Lara had just gotten home from school, and was already changed and picking up her car keys to go out again. Tate was pretty sure he knew exactly where she was going.

"I wanted to pop over to Zane's to see Chloe." She picked up her purse from the kitchen table.

He moved up behind her and wrapped his arms around her waist. "What you really want to do is see the reaction between Chloe and Ellie," he teased, dropping a kiss on the side of her neck. "Are you planning on playing counselor with the two of them?"

Lara turned around in his arms and glared at him. "Of course not. I don't have my advanced degree yet, and I'm not qualified. I just want to see if my sister-in-law and her best friend are okay. Plus, I missed Chloe. What's wrong with that?"

Tate was sorry he said anything because he was afraid his teasing had actually wounded Lara. "Nothing is wrong with caring, sweetheart." He put his arms around her waist. "I was kidding."

If there was one thing among many that he loved about Lara, it was her capacity to give a shit about other people. Granted, sometimes he thought she sacrificed too much. Especially when she offered herself up to a terrorist to save his ornery ass. But that was who Lara was, and there wasn't a damn thing Tate would do to change her. She was fucking perfect in his eyes.

"Then you aren't very funny today," Lara shot back at him huffily.

"I love you," he answered huskily, kissing her on the forehead.

Lara wrapped her arms around his neck. "God, I hate it when you do that."

"What? Love you?"

"Make me forget I was mad with three little words," she whispered against his lips as she rose up on her toes and planted a tender kiss on his mouth.

As usual, touching Lara was all it took to have his cock standing at attention. Hell, even looking at her or hearing her voice could do it. He was hopelessly crazy about his wife. Always had been. Always would be.

"I never meant to piss you off in the first place. It's kind of funny because I have to go pick up Mom. I was coming to talk to you when I saw you getting ready to take off."

Lara leaned back to look at him. "Why?"

Tate shrugged. "So we could all go together to Zane's place. You're not the only one who wants to see Chloe. Mom's bursting with excitement."

His wife lifted a brow. "And you aren't?"

"Okay. I'm curious. Or maybe I'm worried. Hell, Chloe and Ellie have been through so damn much."

Lara cupped his whiskered jaw as she said, "They're strong, Tate. They'll both be fine. Actually, they *are* pretty much fine. I admire both of them."

"Why?" he asked curiously.

"After all they've been through, both of them survived the emotional and physical pain. I'm not sure how well I would have done if it had been me."

Tate looked at her, astonished. "You're the strongest, most kick-ass woman I know. You were an undercover FBI agent, Lara. How much tougher do you want to be?"

"That's just a job, a façade that I needed to keep up for my agency. But I've never known the personal pain either one of them have been through. Yeah, I had a bad relationship, but not like that. Not like them."

"You would have gotten through it," Tate answered staunchly. Maybe Lara had never been tested emotionally like his sister and her best friend had, but he had no doubt Lara could survive anything that came her way. "I would have made damn sure that you did."

"You know, I think you would," Lara said with a laugh. "You're too damn pigheaded to let me spiral down for very long." She paused before adding, "Support is important, and they both had a good guy to lean on when they needed them."

"Gabe helped Chloe a lot," he admitted. In the beginning, he hadn't been too sure that getting involved with another guy so soon was exactly what Chloe needed. But since then, he'd changed his mind. Gabe Walker had ended up being exactly what his little sister needed. "Thank fuck he was a decent man."

"I don't doubt that Zane has helped Ellie, too," Lara answered thoughtfully. "She sounds so much better, like she isn't afraid to go out and live her life again."

Tate nodded. "I guess they've become pretty good friends."

Lara snorted. "If you think that's all they are, you're wrong. Ellie has that certain warmth in her voice when she talks about Zane, that tone a woman has when she adores a certain guy."

He wasn't too sure he understood exactly what his wife was trying to say. Somehow, he couldn't see Zane having a serious relationship. "He's married to his lab, Lara. Hell, we barely see him. He's been that way since we were kids."

"People change, Tate. Maybe he's just been waiting for the right woman. I was married to my career, too. Until some hotshot asshole challenged me, made me realize there was so much more to life than just my job."

Tate wasn't about to admit he was an asshole, even though he probably was, so he answered, "Was that before or after you met me?"

She hit him playfully on the bicep. "Smartass!" Lara wrapped her arms around him and put her head on his shoulder. "You know you make me crazy sometimes. But that's exactly what I need. *You're* exactly what I need."

His arms tightened around her, grateful for the fateful day that Lara had come into his life. He'd never known how lonely he was until he'd found her, and he planned on making sure she never had a reason to stop loving him. "You were what I needed, too, sweetheart. You always will be."

They stayed cuddled together for moment before Lara asked, "What time are we picking up your mom?"

He stepped back and glanced at the clock. "Now," he said with a grin.

"We better move. I'm surprised she hasn't called yet. She has to be excited."

Tate opened the door to let Lara exit, and the cell phone in the pocket of his jeans began to ring.

His wife looked at him and they both smiled before he quickly locked the door and they both sprinted to his vehicle.

Chapter 16

"They're late. Do you think they're okay?" Ellie asked nervously as she looked out the window for the fifth time in the last two minutes, waiting for Chloe and Gabe to come down the driveway.

"Ellie, stop!" Zane insisted from his seat on the living room couch. "Come sit with me. Watching for them won't make them get here any faster."

"I'm fine," she reassured him, knowing she couldn't sit down. Every nerve in her body was jittery with excitement. "I just hope she's not mad about me keeping my rescue a secret. Now I'm not sure if I did the right thing."

Zane rose and grabbed Ellie by the shoulders. "You had the right to do whatever the hell you wanted to do. You were the one who was recovering from an acute traumatic incident. It was your call, and none of anybody else's business, Ell. You had a right to do whatever made you comfortable then."

"But she's my best friend," she answered woefully. "Maybe it was selfish, but I didn't want anyone to see me that way. I needed some time. And I didn't want her to come rushing back because of me."

"So you had the right to recover in peace," Zane answered reasonably. "You needed to just worry about yourself. For God's sake, you almost died."

"You didn't let me recover in peace," she reminded him with a small smile. "You were stubborn, manipulating, and bossy."

"Only about you staying safe," he grumbled. "I wanted you to be happy again. Just because you had the right to be alone doesn't mean that you should have been."

"I needed you," Ellie relented as she put her arms around him. "I just didn't want to admit it. You saved me in more ways than one, you know. I really had nobody with Chloe gone. Yeah, I've lived in Rocky Springs all my life, but I guess I never realized how few real friends I really had. Not that it matters, because Chloe makes up for that. She's as real as they get."

"You. Have. Me." Zane wrapped his arms around her waist. "And really good friends are hard to find, especially when somebody works as much as you do. When you aren't doing things for me, you're working to build your online business. I spent so much time in the lab that I never developed a ton of great friends either. I have work associates, but when it comes right down to people who would stand beside me if I needed them, there's pretty much just my family."

"You have me now." Ellie repeated his words back to him.

"Believe me, I know how damn lucky I am to have you," Zane answered sincerely, his eyes heated.

Ellie blinked back tears, something she did often when one of Zane's honest confessions about her touched her soul. *Really, was he that lucky to have a woman like her, a female who had caused him more work than joy?*

She thought for a moment, stopping herself and her negative thoughts. Despite her remembered pain, there was so much joy in her life with Zane, and both of them were happy. The hard times were still difficult to deal with, but the good things outweighed the bad now. In fact, sometimes Ellie thought her life couldn't be more perfect. Yes, sometimes an occasional nightmare or old habits still plagued her, but for the most part, Zane had helped set her free.

Her life was different. *She* was different, all because Zane Colter had come into her life. Even before her kidnapping, her world had been very small. He'd helped her widen her universe, and no matter what happened them in the future, she'd always be grateful to him.

I love you!

Although Ellie desperately wanted to say those words as she looked into his tempestuous gray gaze, she hesitated. They were a couple for now, but Zane had never talked about being in love. Did he even believe in love, or just monogamy? Frankly, Ellie believed Zane was her soulmate, the man she was always meant to be with. But she accepted a man of science was probably not going to agree with a theory like hers.

The doorbell chimed suddenly, dragging Ellie from her thoughts.

"Chloe," she whispered reverently, like her best friend was a superstar.

"I'll get it," Zane offered.

"No. I'm fine. We'll go together."

Zane twined his fingers around hers, offering his silent support as they strolled to the front door. He flipped the deadbolt open, and the heavy wooden door swung open.

There in front of her was a smiling, happy Chloe, looking more amazing than she ever had before. Not that Chloe had ever looked bad, but she seemed to have a glow to her that had always been missing.

Ellie stared at her incredulously, and then…she lost it.

Reaching out, she wrapped an arm around Chloe's neck and pulled her inside the door with a sob. "Oh, God. I didn't think I'd ever see you again."

Ellie's tears flowed freely as the women became locked in a hug so exuberant that they both dropped to their knees.

"I'm so sorry, Ellie. I'm so damn sorry," Chloe choked out through her tears.

She hugged her best friend harder. "It's over now. I'm here. It doesn't matter."

Now, Ellie was glad she hadn't told Chloe she was alive. She could only imagine her reaction if she'd seen her during her walking-skeleton days when she couldn't even walk by herself. With her huge heart, the images would have haunted Chloe forever.

"I was so afraid I'd never see you again," Chloe muttered in between her heavy sobs of relief.

"I love you so much!" Chloe exclaimed.

"I love you, too," Ellie responded immediately.

Neither woman really noticed as the men in the room lifted them back to their feet, both guys looking concerned, their eyes suspiciously damp. Neither man could look away from the reunion. All they could do was share the joy of two women who were so damn happy to be together again.

Finally, Chloe pulled back and took Ellie by the shoulders. "Let me look at you. Oh, my God. You look fantastic. You lost weight, and I love your hair shorter."

Ellie smiled at Chloe, determined to never mention exactly why she was at a normal weight. She wasn't going to say a thing about her shorter hair, either. Her hair had grown, but it would take years to get the length she'd had before. Then again, she wasn't sure she even wanted that anymore. She liked the shorter style and the ease of taking care of it.

Clasping her friend's arms, Ellie did her own inspection of Chloe, noticing how worry-free she looked right now except for the stream of tears flowing down her face. "You look happy," she said simply. It summed up exactly what she saw.

"I am. Oh, let me introduce you to Gabe, my husband."

Untangling herself from Chloe, Ellie looked at the tall, dark, and handsome man beside her friend. "We've crossed paths a few times. Congratulations, Gabe. You got the most wonderful wife you could ever want," Ellie told him with a wink as she held out her hand.

Gabe nodded and smiled at her as he shook her hand. "Don't I know it," he replied with a slight drawl. "If I forget, she reminds me."

Chloe tapped him on the arm. "I certainly do not," she countered, mocking indignantly.

Drawing back her arm, Ellie noticed that Gabe's smile went all the way to his eyes, making them twinkle with mischief. God, her best friend *had* found the perfect man. Ellie had a feeling that Gabe and Chloe laughed a lot.

She watched as Gabe and Zane shook hands and slapped each other on the back.

Chloe turned to her brother and gave him a gigantic hug.

"How was the extended honeymoon?" Zane asked, apparently asking the question to lighten the mood. "Come on into the living room." He led the way.

Ellie and Chloe followed, their arms locked together like they were afraid to let go.

"It was amazing," Chloe gushed. "But none of the trip was better than coming home. It still seems surreal to me that Ellie is here. I guess it will take a while for me to get used to having her back."

The two women took a seat on the couch and turned to face each other.

"Are you really okay?" Chloe asked hesitantly.

Ellie nodded. "I won't bullshit you and tell you I don't have some lingering problems, but I'm working through them. Zane saved my life."

"Were you cold? Did that bastard feed you? Did he hurt you?" There was a desperate note in Chloe's voice.

"I was cold, and he left me very little food and water, but enough to last until Zane found me." Ellie wasn't going to lie to Chloe. But she hoped her friend didn't ask any more questions.

Both men had taken a seat in one of the chairs across from the couch, and Chloe's eyes searched out Zane. "Thank you. But I still want to kill you for not telling me she was alive."

"Don't," Ellie interrupted. "Please don't blame anyone but me. I wanted some time to get my head together. Zane and Gabe respected that. If you're angry, it's all on me. I asked them not to tell. I think we both needed our time to heal."

"I'm not mad at you, Ellie, and I'm really not angry with Zane. How could I be? He saved you."

The intercom at the gate chimed, and Ellie looked at Zane, perplexed. "Is somebody else coming over?"

Zane rolled his eyes. "Are you kidding? They'll all be here. Maybe I should leave the front gate open."

"Who?"

"My family. Did you really think my brothers and Mom would miss this?"

Chloe squealed with delight as she jumped up to answer the intercom. "I don't know how to let them in, but I'm glad they're here. I just wished they'd given us more time to talk."

Honestly, Ellie was relieved. Although she wanted to have some quiet time with Chloe, she wasn't sure she was ready for some of the things her friend might ask.

Zane rose, not bothering to answer the intercom. He just buzzed the vehicle in.

Before the car reached the end of the driveway, he had to let another vehicle pass through the gate. "Hell, I hope some of them rode together," he grumbled as he went to answer the door.

Ellie knew Zane got his wish as she saw Marcus and Blake enter together, and then Tate, Lara, and Chloe's mother a few minutes later.

Aileen had brought dinner for everyone from the resort, so the guys unloaded the stuff from Lara's car.

As the party moved away from the living room, Zane caught her arm on the way into the kitchen. "Baby, I hate to do this right now, but Sean just called. He's having some emergency at the lab."

"Today? It's the weekend." Ellie knew that some of the research staff worked weekends, but rarely the guys at the top. Sean was usually off with Elena, and he wasn't required to do any weekends.

"He said Elena left him, and he wanted to take his mind off her. So he went to work because he was starting to have some luck on one of our projects. But some of the equipment isn't working. I have to have it up and running by Monday morning."

"Then, go," Ellie urged. "I'll stay here and visit with Chloe."

Zane nodded reluctantly. "I always want you with me, but I'm not about to drag you away from here right now. I'll be back by tomorrow."

Ellie wrapped her arms around Zane's neck and kissed him, right there in front of his family. He deepened the embrace, running his hands through her hair and devouring her mouth until she was breathless.

"I'll miss you," Ellie told him earnestly.

"I'll miss you, too. Have fun with Chloe."

He was gone as quickly as he'd approached her, leaving a whole lot of questioning expressions behind. Ellie looked around, and everybody was staring.

The only one who didn't look surprised was Marcus.

"We're seeing each other," Ellie mumbled nervously.

Marcus crossed his arms in front of him with an evil grin. "I sure as hell hope so. If not, I'm going to have to talk to him about friendship etiquette."

Chloe threw herself at Ellie with enthusiasm and gave Ellie a big hug. "I'm so happy for both of you. Thank you."

Ellie hugged her back. "For what?"

"For making my brother happy. I could tell he cared about you from his expression. I'm so glad the feeling is mutual."

"Way mutual," Ellie said laughingly.

"I know you had a crush on him when you were younger, and I always wondered if there wasn't still something there. You asked about him a lot."

Ellie's cheeks reddened. "I'm sorry. I wasn't fishing for information. I just…"

Okay. Maybe she had been wanting to know what Zane was doing, who he was seeing, and any other information she could get. But it hadn't been intentional.

"It's fine. He grilled me for information about you, too," Chloe reassured her. "I'm just happy you're together now. Do you love him?"

Her best friend's question took her off-guard. Finally, she nodded. "With all of my heart. I've wanted to tell him so many times, but I didn't want to ruin what we have."

"You won't. He loves you, too," Chloe responded nonchalantly.

Ellie wanted to ask how she knew that, and if she really thought it was true, but her friend got distracted by her mother dragging her to the kitchen with her to talk and catch up.

Chloe mouthed, *"Talk later."*

Ellie nodded, and then turned to Blake, who was trying to ask where Zane had gone. Her heart clenched as she explained that he'd had to go to the lab.

Pathetically, she missed him already.

Chapter 17

The impromptu family gathering went on for hours, with plenty of laughing, eating, and drinking while the whole clan was together catching up. Aileen was happy, saying that it was rare for them all to be in Rocky Springs at the same time. She'd also implied that she was happy that Zane had somebody to pull himself out of the lab from time to time.

It was late by the time Ellie got the phone call that was about to make her entire world come crashing down on her.

Most of the family had settled into the family room because it was bigger, when Ellie heard the telltale sound of Zane's ringtone sounding on her cell. Springing to her feet, she scrambled out to the kitchen and quickly rummaged in her purse for the phone.

"Hello," she finally answered breathlessly.

"Ellie?" The voice wasn't Zane's. Ellie was confused for a moment before she recognized it.

"Sean? What's going on? Where is Zane?" Her heart started to beat rapidly, knowing that if Zane let Sean use his phone, something was wrong.

"He's here, but he's tied up. Literally. I couldn't say whether he appreciates me holding a gun to his head, but I don't give a shit."

Ellie's heart fell as she sensed Sean's mood, the sound of mania in his voice. She'd experienced this before, and it hadn't turned out well. "Why? Sean, why would you do that when he was the one who chose you to be in charge of the research lab? He hired you, he was your mentor after he put you in a position of power at the lab."

"You think I'm a boss? Hell, no. I don't have the money Zane has, and I never will unless I make my own luck. Your boyfriend was born with a platinum spoon in his mouth. I wasn't. The only thing I ever wanted was Elena, and she left me for a wealthier man. I want her back. In order to do that, I need money and a way to become wealthy enough to get Elena back. And you're going to get it for me."

Ellie walked into the family room, every member of the Colter family going quiet as they looked at her pale complexion. She put a finger to her lips as a sign to stay silent.

"I'll bring it to you if you just promise me you won't hurt Zane. Please."

Tate got up and came over to where she was standing on the phone, turning it so he could listen in with her.

Sean grunted. "That's not all I want. Zane's been doing some private research, an independent project that doesn't belong to the lab. I want the research."

"I-I don't even know where it is. What is it?"

"He has an underground lab there. I need the laptop he keeps down there."

"I don't—"

Tate quickly put a finger over his mouth and shook his head. *Was he telling her not to let Sean know that she didn't have access to the lab?* Evidently, that was exactly what he seemed to be saying.

"I don't know exactly where it is, but I'll find it," she told Sean adamantly, realizing Tate was right. If she admitted she couldn't get what Sean wanted, he might kill Zane.

"Make it fast. I want you here by ten o'clock tomorrow morning or I'll waste your boyfriend. Then you can see how it feels to lose somebody you love. Maybe then you'll understand," Sean rambled.

"It's the weekend. The money may not be accessible," she stalled.

"They're Colters." Sean spit out the name like it was vile. "Those bastards can get anything they want. I want a million dollars in unmarked bills, *and* the laptop from Zane's home lab."

"Is anybody else there in the lab with you?" Ellie saw Tate nodding at her out of the corner of her eye.

"Nope. Everybody took the weekend off. It's just me and the asshole who distracted my woman, turned her head with money."

Ellie's hands were shaking, so Tate took the phone from her, keeping it in the same position. She wanted to argue with Sean, tell him Elena had never been worth all of this, that Zane had never had the slightest interest in her, but she didn't. Zane had never encouraged the woman. Ellie had seen that firsthand. But it was impossible to reason with a man who had gone off the deep end. Unfortunately, she'd learned that the hard way.

While she was grateful that Sean couldn't hurt anybody else in the lab, she was terrified for Zane. "I want to talk to him. Put Zane on the phone so I know he's still alive."

She heard a scuffle and then Zane's desperate voice. "Ellie, don't come here. Call the police and let them handle it. He's not going to let either one of us go. He'll just kill us both."

Sean must have gagged Zane again, because it was quiet as he came back on the phone. "He's wrong. If you follow my instructions, I'll let him go. I'll have the means to become a very rich man with the money and his research. If you bring in the police or I see one police car sitting in front of this building, it's over. Bring the stuff by morning and come alone. If you don't, your boyfriend is dead."

Ellie panicked as she heard the distinctive sound of a dead line. "Sean! Wait! Please!"

Tate clicked out of the call and put her phone down on one of the tables in the family room.

"Disgruntled employee, I take it?" Tate asked.

Ellie quickly explained everything she knew about Sean and Elena to Zane's family, which was really very little. Then, she shared everything that had happened on the phone call.

"So it's some fortune-seeking bitch who isn't even worth it," Marcus commented disgustedly.

"I don't know what to do," Ellie admitted. "I don't even know how to access Zane's lab here. He always meant to take me down there, but we never got a chance before we left for Denver."

"You know the project he's working on?" Blake questioned.

"Yes. Not in depth, but he said he's been working on some vaccines for some worldwide diseases. Since it was going to take years, he started the project on the side. I don't know how close he is to being finished, but I know that putting that research into the wrong hands could be disastrous if making money is the only objective to wanting the studies. Zane didn't want pharmaceuticals. He wanted prevention. That's why he kept it a secret. He wanted to take the research all the way to vaccines, and he's meticulous about thorough research and replication before he acts on a discovery. He probably felt he could share the project information with Sean. He's the director at the Denver office. Zane's information should have been safe with Sean."

"Where's his lab?" Tate asked urgently.

"Underground. But it has security."

Tate grinned. "Not a problem. Just lead me there." More seriously, he asked, "Marcus, can you round up the money?"

The eldest Colter was already texting. "I'm working on it."

Ellie led Tate to the entrance of the underground lab and slid the front panel aside. Tate gently pushed his way in, looking at the security device on the door.

"It's a fingerprint scanner," he observed, playing with a few of the mechanisms on the heavy door.

"So we can't get in without Zane's print?"

"Generally, no. Not unless he reset the door to accept your prints, too."

"He didn't," Ellie said sadly, wishing she had pushed more to see what Zane was doing in the lab. "I don't think he wanted me down there alone. He said there were too many harmful substances there."

"Don't worry, Ellie. I can breach the system. I just need to get some tools, and it might take me a while. But no security system is unbreakable if you know enough about them."

Ellie knew that Tate was probably one of the best people to have around if she needed somebody to break and enter. "Okay. What else can I do? Should I report this to the police?"

"Hell, no," Blake commented as he came to check out what Tate was doing. "They'd have police swarming the building. The minute this asshole sees a cop car, Zane's chances of getting out alive aren't good."

"He's right," Marcus remarked, having followed Blake into the hallway. "The cops are going to do what they're trained to do. That means SWAT teams, hostage negotiators, and all of the other things that will get Zane killed. Once Tate breaks into the lab, we'll handle this."

"I'm going with you," Ellie said stubbornly. "He told me to bring it, and if he sees you guys, it could turn out badly. Besides, I know the building. I know how to get in without being detected. I have the codes for the alarms, and I know where the lab area and offices are located."

"You're not going," Tate said flatly. "Zane would never forgive us if something happened to you. Christ! You've just recovered from being kidnapped."

"If you don't take me with you, I'll show up there anyway," Ellie argued. There was no way she was staying behind.

"I'm going, too," Blake insisted.

"Neither one of you are trained in hostage situations. Just let Tate and I deal with it so nobody else gets hurt," Marcus said gruffly.

Ellie crossed her arms and glared at all three men. "I have to go. He's expecting to see me. How do you think you're going to explain when I don't show up? If you catch him off-guard, we might have a chance."

"She has a point," Tate ventured. "But you know Zane's going to be pissed."

Blake shrugged. "Better angry than dead."

"I don't like it," Marcus rumbled. "It's too dangerous for Ellie."

Frustrated, Ellie turned around and went back into the family room, hoping for some backup. All three men followed.

"It's not that we don't think you can do it, Ellie," Tate said as he entered the family room with the others right behind him.

"Then tell me what it is, because I'm going to be there whether you like it or not. It's Zane's only hope right now. If he sees you two, he could kill Zane." She took a deep breath and tried to calm down.

"You have to understand that we can't put your life in danger. I would kill anybody who let Lara come to any harm, including one of my brothers," Tate answered irritably.

"I'm going, too," Lara informed her husband matter-of-factly. "You could use another skilled professional with a gun."

"Like hell you will," Tate argued angrily, giving Lara a warning glance.

Ellie saw Chloe sitting on the couch with a crying Aileen, trying to comfort her mother. All this arguing wasn't making this any easier on Aileen or the rest of the family.

"Stop!" Ellie raised her voice to be heard over all the noise. Now wasn't the time for debating. "I think all of you need to understand that nothing will keep me from being in that building tomorrow morning. Zane saved my life. He never gave up on me, even though he should have." She hesitated before adding, "Since he never gave up on me, I'm never giving up on him. I'd rather die trying than live in this world without him."

Tears were streaming down her face as she finished her speech.

"We know you care about him," Blake said quietly.

"I. Love. Him." Ellie put emphasis on each word. "I love him more than anything else in this world."

God, she wished she had told Zane how she felt. Now, it seemed so petty to be worried about his reaction.

"Are we going to make a plan, or are we going to sit here and argue?" Marcus asked drily.

They all decided that a plan was the best option.

Chapter 18

Zane knew he was going to die. It was just a question of *when* Sean decided to off him. The only consolation he had was that at least Ellie wasn't here with him, and he knew his brothers would keep her safe.

It had been a long night, Sean keeping Zane in a state of semi-consciousness so the guy could sleep.

Like it wasn't enough that he was tied to a chair in Sean's office with so much overkill that Zane couldn't possibly get loose. And dammit, he'd tried. Over and over again. The moment he started making too much noise, Sean would wake and bash him over the head again. Thankfully, Zane could hear his employee snoring from his office chair behind him now.

Really, he found it pretty ironic that he was being held captive in an office he owned and had given to Sean when he'd hired him not all that long ago. It was a damn nice office, too. Now, he regretted not putting his director in some crappy cubbyhole somewhere instead of granting him an executive office as nice as his own.

Zane tried not to make a sound as his head began to clear. He wanted to be awake and conscious in case the police arrived, to see if he could do anything to help keep himself alive. Honestly, he'd expected police intervention way before now. It was definitely morning, and by looking at the sun rising through the window, it was well beyond dawn.

Fuck! He hoped to hell that Ellie wasn't planning on carrying through on Sean's demands. The bastard would kill them both in a heartbeat if she came walking into the building with the stuff Sean wanted. Zane's heart chilled.

Whatever Sean's issues were, they weren't with Zane. He'd just become his employee's fixation, a target that didn't really exist.

Why did I never see the signs? How was he able to hide this side of himself for so long?

Zane knew it happened. Hell, he'd just seen a news story about a father, husband and seemingly normal man with no criminal record who just went off one day, killing multiple people in a mass shooting.

Maybe Elena's apparently final desertion had set Sean off, but Zane had no doubt that Sean's mental issues had always existed and had been hidden away, just waiting for the right reason to go psychotic. The guy might have a brilliant scientific mind, but in other areas of his brain, there were definitely some major problems.

Turning his head slowly, he looked at the clock.

Almost nine!

He was getting nervous, worried about the fact that the police still hadn't showed. Was Ellie really going to try to bring what Sean wanted? *Please God, no!*

Not possible. I never got her access to my lab in Rocky Springs.

However, Zane knew that Ellie would have needed to work with his family if she wanted the money Sean wanted, and his brothers could be downright dangerous. With Tate and Marcus's skills, Zane didn't doubt they might try something themselves. It was the only explanation for why the police weren't here.

God dammit! The last thing I want is for any of them to get hurt.

He would probably have a better chance of getting out of this alive if Tate and Marcus were planning something together. Truth was, he wanted to live. Zane didn't want to leave Ellie on this Earth alone, and he wanted to be around for her. They hadn't had enough time yet. He wasn't ready yet.

I never told her how much I love her.

That was Zane's deepest regret. Maybe he wasn't a romantic guy, and maybe he hadn't been all that good at telling Ellie exactly how he felt. But damn! How hard was it to tell her that he loved her, that he'd do damn near anything to see her smile?

Obviously, it was difficult or he would have already told her. He hadn't wanted to scare her off by pouring his heart out all at once. Now, he wished he would have just taken the chance.

Sean's snoring suddenly stopped, and Zane quickly closed his eyes. Better to look like he was still unconscious until something happened, and he knew something would. He knew his brothers, and they weren't going to leave Zane's fate to the police, especially when Sean had threatened to kill him the minute he saw a police car.

Something was going to happen. He knew his family was up to something. He just wished he knew exactly what they had planned.

Ellie waited long enough for Tate, Marcus, and Lara to gain access to the ventilation system. She'd let them into the building through the delivery entrance with her key before coding in the numbers that would stop the alarm system in the area, and relocking the back entrance after the three of them were in place.

Once their plan had been worked out the night before, Blake had been excluded because what they were doing wasn't exactly the way the government would approve of handling the situation, and Blake had a senator's seat to consider. He hadn't been happy, but he'd finally bowed out, mostly because he didn't want to be a hindrance since he had no experience in law enforcement.

I have to be patient. I have to give them time to get through the ventilation system.

Ellie hadn't slept, but she was far from tired. Her nerves were on edge, and her hands were shaky as she made her way to the front entrance of the building. She knew she'd be lying if she said she wasn't afraid, but it was Zane's life she was afraid for right now.

What if he's already dead?

She had to stop and take a deep breath, clear her mind of negative thoughts. There'd be no functioning the way she needed to if she panicked.

A cold chill ran down her spine, and she instantly knew she was being watched. The window in Sean's office looked over the entrance, and Ellie was positive he was scrutinizing her every move.

Hefting the duffel bag over her shoulder so he could see that she was carrying a bag and a laptop under her other arm, she unlocked the door of Colter Labs and stepped inside.

With a glance at the alarm panel, she noticed that the system for the main building was off. Sean had either never reset the office and reception alarms, or he'd just shut them off before she entered.

Her phone rang, and she startled, nearly dropping Zane's laptop. Hurriedly, she sat the bag and the computer on the receptionist desk and pulled her phone out of the pocket of her jeans.

She looked at the caller ID before she answered. "I have what you want. Now I want a trade." Her voice was surprisingly firm. Anger that Sean had brought Zane into his crazy game was fueling her courage right now.

"Come up to my office alone," Sean warned.

"I *am* alone," she shot back at him. "I'm on my way, and I want to see Zane."

"He's here, and he's not very happy right now," Sean replied cheerfully.

"What did you do to him?" Ellie asked furiously, only to find that the line was now silent.

"Dammit!" She shoved her phone back in her pocket and gathered up the items on the desk, and then made her way to the elevators that led to the offices.

By now, Tate, Lara, and Marcus should be in position. Ellie wasn't sure what had finally made Tate relent and bring Lara along with him. But Ellie had heard him remind his wife of her promise before he'd gone into the building, so Ellie knew Tate didn't believe Lara should be anywhere near the dangerous situation.

Ellie took some deep breaths before the lift stopped at the floor where Sean's office was located, trying to keep as calm as possible. Her greatest fear was that she couldn't save Zane.

He never gave up on me. I won't give up on him.

The words had become her mantra, her strength. She'd give her life in exchange for Zane's in a heartbeat; she was just afraid that she wouldn't have the chance.

Sean's office door was open, and Ellie felt her heart hammering against her chest as she walked into the space slowly, frantically looking for Zane. "Where is he?" she asked, feeling like she wanted to smash the evil smile off Sean's face as he greeted her at the door.

"I'll take those," he growled menacingly, snatching the duffel bag and laptop from her arms.

Her eyes caught sight of one of Sean's office chairs moving, a pair of hiking boots flat on the floor. "Zane!" She ignored Sean, who was rifling through the bag to make sure it contained real money, and ran to the chair.

Fury coursed through her body as she saw how he was literally tied from neck to knee into the chair, blood streaming from his head, his face bruised. "You bastard," Ellie turned and cursed at Sean. "You hurt him."

"I didn't say I wouldn't have a little fun," Sean answered nonchalantly as he pulled his handgun from his waistband and pointed it in their direction.

"You said you wanted a trade." She tried not to flinch as Sean carelessly waved the gun in the air before retraining it toward her and Zane. She kept Zane's back to Sean while she faced him, her body beside Zane's chair. If Sean was going to shoot Zane, he'd have to come through her first.

"Surely you aren't that ignorant, Ellie," Sean answered. "If I let you go, then what? I'd be on the run for the rest of my life. That's not the way I have things planned. I kill both of you, and by the time they find your bodies, I'll be on my way out of the country. I have a charter waiting, and I can sell scientific discoveries anywhere. A million dollars can go a long way to setting me up where I'll be safe."

"Zane's family will hunt you down like a hound dog on the scent of a rabbit. They'd chase your ass to the end of the Earth if they had to," Ellie hissed.

"There are places that even the Colters can't reach. Besides, they can't prove that you two didn't have a little domestic dispute and ended up with a murder/suicide situation. I can make it look that way."

"They already know you have him as a hostage."

"They'd have to prove I killed you both. Believe me, I'll cover my tracks."

Sean raised the gun to follow through on his murderous intentions. Then, everything happened at once.

Ellie slammed into Zane's chair with her body, pushing it so hard that they both landed on the other side of the room as Sean's gunshot exploded, hitting the area where she and Zane had just been positioned, shattering the glass in the office window in the process.

From her vantage point on the floor, Ellie tried to take in the situation. Evidently, Marcus must have let go of the heavy metal grille to the vent system, the hit to the head disorientating Sean, before Marcus came down right on top of him and subdued him. Tate followed, dropping into the fray. Lara swung off to the side, landing on her feet on the carpeted floor, and drew her handgun.

Not having a single doubt that Marcus, Tate, and Lara could handle Sean, Ellie turned her attention to Zane, finding some scissors and a pocket knife in Sean's desk drawers to start cutting the bindings.

She pulled the tape off his mouth first, which, in hindsight, was a big mistake.

"What in the fuck did you think you were doing? I told you to call the police. You had to have known he wasn't likely to let either

one of us go. Why did you do this, Ellie? I asked you not to do it."
Zane was furious, but there was also fear in his eyes.

Ellie had cut through the substantial twine and rope around
Zane's body and worked through some of the knots. "I swear if you
say another word, I'll put the tape back on your mouth again," she
warned as she put some muscle into cutting one of his ties.

Out of the corner of her eye, she could see that Marcus and Tate
had easily subdued Sean. Police officers barreled through the door,
and she heard Tate mumble, "Right on time," as the officers took
over custody of the struggling madman.

"Just tell me why? I could fucking handle that asshole killing me,
but not you," Zane growled.

Ellie sawed and jerked on a particularly tight piece of rope as she
answered, "Well, I *couldn't* handle him killing *you*. It would have
been like he killed me, too. Even though you aren't being particularly
pleasant right now, I love your stubborn ass, Zane Colter, and I wasn't
about to give up on you. You never gave up on me." Ellie spoke her
mantra again, hoping it would be the last time she needed to say it.

The rope finally gave, and she was able to finally free Zane from
his prison. He had to be sore. He hadn't been able to move all night.

Marcus, Tate, and Lara ran over to Zane the moment the police
took Sean out of the office in handcuffs.

"You okay?" Marcus asked, frowning as he saw the blood coming
from Zane's head and the bruises on his face.

"Did you just tell me that you love me?" Zane questioned, his
gaze focused on Ellie.

"Yes. I'm tired of not saying it, so I'll say it again. I love you, Zane
Colter, and you couldn't expect me to sit and do nothing."

"I love you, too," Zane replied huskily. "Not telling you that was
my only regret."

Ellie's heart soared as she looked at him. "Marcus asked if you
were okay?" she reminded him, since he'd completely ignored his
brother. "Can you stand?"

"Of course," Zane said arrogantly as he started to rise from
his chair.

Luckily, Tate and Marcus were there to catch Zane's body as he fell, the two of them laying him gently on the ground.

"Sorry. I guess I got dizzy," Zane mumbled, his eyes closed.

Marcus probed Zane's injuries. "He has some pretty bad gashes and lumps. I think we need an ambulance. He probably has a concussion."

"Already on the way," Lara answered as she stuffed her phone back in her pocket, obviously having already called for help.

"I'm going to be so pissed when I'm not so damn dizzy," Zane muttered. "Ellie and Lara definitely shouldn't have been here, and neither should any of my family. You should have just called the police. And how in the hell did you get my laptop?"

"You have one brother who was Special Forces, another who is a CIA operative, and a sister-in-law who is an ex-FBI agent. If none of us could get to your laptop, it would have been pretty damn sad," Lara told Zane in a gently joking tone.

Zane scowled without opening his eyes, which made Ellie smile. She knew it probably annoyed him that his security wasn't completely foolproof.

A moment later, he opened his eyes, squinting at everyone kneeling beside him. "Ellie loves me. Doesn't that make me a lucky bastard?"

"He's getting goofy," Tate observed.

"In this case, I rather think he knows exactly what he's saying, and I'd have to agree," Marcus said calmly as he looked at Ellie. "Thanks for what you did. We couldn't have pulled this off without you, and you certainly didn't need to do it."

She smiled at Marcus, knowing there was much more to this brother of Zane's who liked to think he was detached and only cared about superficial things like fast cars and nice possessions. "Yes, I did have to do it. I love him, too."

Lara and Tate smiled, and Marcus gave Ellie a satisfied look. "I know."

Zane moved his hand, and Ellie caught it, twining his fingers with hers. "Hold on. The ambulance is here."

"I'll be fine," Zane argued, moving like he wanted to get up.

In unison, Tate and Marcus pushed Zane back down as the paramedics came to take a look at him.

Ellie stepped back to make room for the medical personnel and Lara wrapped her arm around her shoulders supportively. "He'll be okay. I've discovered all of the Colter brothers have hard heads. He took some pretty hard blows, but he'll recover."

Ellie looked at the shattered window and then back at Zane. "It could have been worse, I suppose."

"That was quick thinking to get yourself and Zane clear of any misfire," Lara told her quietly.

"Instinct," Ellie said, brushing Lara's compliment off.

"Love," Lara countered with a smile.

Ellie grinned back at her. "He loves me. Zane really loves me." Still giddy with relief and Zane's declaration, she felt a little bit silly herself.

"I know," Lara repeated Marcus's words. "Another single Colter guy off the market."

"There's still Blake and Marcus," Ellie reminded her as she and Lara followed the paramedics once they'd secured Zane on a gurney and were in motion.

"Blake is married to his position as a senator, and Marcus..." Lara's voice trailed off for a few seconds before she concluded, "What woman would ever put up with him? She'd have to be able to kick his ass."

Ellie chuckled as they went down the elevator. She grasped Zane's hand and felt him squeeze her fingers weakly.

Right now, there was only one Colter man she'd gladly take off the bachelor market for good. Never again would she hide the way she felt about him. Life was too short. If she hadn't learned that from her own experience, she definitely had from this incident.

Ellie felt like she'd waited a lifetime for Zane, and she wasn't about to wait any longer.

Chapter 19

Ellie was glad that Zane only had an overnight stay in the hospital, because he was a terrible patient. She found it slightly amusing that he'd been so adamant about her waiting when she'd wanted to leave the hospital following her ordeal. But he obviously didn't think the same caution was necessary when it came to him. He was complaining about needing to stay the night from the moment the doctor had deemed it necessary to watch him for the first twenty-four hours because of his concussion.

He'd gone home with staples in his head, and a whole lot of family around constantly, every one of them worried about him.

Three days after he was released from the hospital, Chloe and Gabe stopped by. Gabe and Zane were watching a ball game on TV while Chloe and Ellie tried to work through everything that had happened to them.

"Sometimes it seems like it happened so long ago," Ellie mused as she sat at the kitchen table, talking to Chloe. "I know I still have issues from what happened, but my memories are slowly fading away. Maybe because I've had so many good memories with your brother to replace the bad ones."

Chloe sighed. "Sometimes I feel that way, too. Having you back is still fresh, but the damage that was done by James is being obliterated by my life with Gabe."

"You're really happy?" Ellie was hesitant to ask because it was pretty evident that Gabe and Chloe adored each other.

"Very. He saved my life. Not in the way that Zane saved yours, but without his support and love, I'm not sure where I'd be right now." Chloe hesitated before asking, "So when is the wedding?"

Ellie shook her head. "Not anytime soon. We haven't discussed it."

Chloe laughed. "It will be soon. Zane never has waited around for something he wanted. Now that he knows you love him, he's going to want to see his ring on your finger."

"I'm not in any hurry," Ellie said quickly.

"I am," Chloe argued. "I want to be a matron of honor before I end up pregnant."

Ellie gaped at her best friend. "Are you trying?"

"Not yet. But we're planning on it. Gabe wants me to wait until I'm ready. But I think I'm pretty much getting there. I want to have our first child soon. Hopefully we'll have more than one."

Ellie could easily see Chloe as a mother. She'd be amazing. "I'd better be one of the first to know when you get pregnant."

"You know you will be. I won't be able to wait to tell you. But in the meantime, I'm looking forward to your wedding."

"Don't hold your breath," Ellie warned. Although she and Zane professed their love every day, she wasn't sure he was ready to make that leap just yet.

Chloe rose as Gabe and Zane came into the room. "Ready to go?"

"Whenever you are," Gabe answered agreeably. "We couldn't watch the game anymore. We were getting an ass whooping."

"I have to go anyway. I need to check on a couple of the horses," Chloe reminded her spouse.

Ellie watched her best friend talk to her husband. The two of them so obviously belonged together. She could see the unspoken understanding between the two of them, the love that seemed to radiate from both of their souls.

They all said their good-byes as Gabe and Chloe departed, leaving the house quiet again.

"Thank God," Zane pronounced as he closed and locked the door. "It seems like we haven't had a minute alone since I got back from the hospital."

They had received a lot of visitors, mostly his concerned family. "You're supposed to be recovering."

Zane still had stitches and staples in his head, but he was healing quickly, most of the bruises on his face already gone.

"I *am* recovered," he argued, heading back toward the family room.

Ellie followed him. "No, you're not. Sit down and I'll make you something for dinner."

"I'd rather have you," Zane rasped, catching her before she could go back to the kitchen. "I need you, Ellie. I need you so damn much that I can't wait any longer. I want to tell you I love you while I'm deep inside you."

Ellie fell into his pleading gaze, her body aching for his possession. She'd wanted the same thing, but hadn't wanted to delay his recovery. "I don't just love the sex, Zane. I. Love. You."

"I don't just want the sex either. I want you, Ellie."

His expression was pleading, and she wasn't certain she could deny him. Taking his hand, she led him toward the couch. Flipping the button on his jeans, she made short work of his clothing, finally pushing him down on the sofa completely, spectacularly naked.

She tried not to get distracted by his perfectly sculpted body, determined not to let him impede his recovery. But it wasn't easy when a man looked as hot as Zane Colter, and he was sitting within touching distance without a stitch of clothing on his muscular, perfect body.

Strangely, the fact that he was fantastically hot didn't intimidate her at all. Maybe it was because she knew that even if he wasn't so irresistibly gorgeous, she'd still want him just as much as she did right now.

"You behave. I'm doing all the work," she told him sternly.

His hungry eyes watched her, his cock fully erect as he blatantly stared at her as she divested herself of her clothing one piece at a time.

Ellie still couldn't believe that Zane looked at her like she was one of the highest paid models in the world, attractive to him in every way. He never seemed to see any of her body flaws, or that she was only passably attractive. When he looked at her, Zane saw her through the eyes of a man who was in love with her. *That* was a miracle to her, and her eyes grew moist with tears because he loved her exactly as she was: something she'd always hoped for, but never thought to find.

"You're killing me," Zane groaned, watching as she shimmied out of the last item of her clothing: her skimpy thong panties.

She moved toward him, her fingers itching to touch him, to reassure herself that even though he had some lingering injuries, he was going to be okay.

Dropping to the floor, she knelt between his thighs. Placing her palms on his shoulders, she slowly let them slide down his muscular chest and ripped abs, savoring the warmth and hardness of his body. Finally, she grasped his rigid cock, stroking the soft, silken feel of him. So hard, but so incredibly smooth at the same time.

"Ellie, I'm not going to last long if you don't stop," Zane cautioned her in a raspy voice.

"I don't care," she answered in a sultry tone. "This isn't about endurance. This is all about how much I love you, how I know I could have lost you. This is all about us."

She lowered her head and flicked the drop of moisture from the head of his cock, stopping to enjoy his essence before she slowly lowered her mouth down on him. Her pussy flooded with moisture as she heard his erotic groan, her body already aroused just from touching Zane, knowing he was experiencing so much pleasure from her touch.

He speared his hands into her hair, stroking the curls and guiding her while she sucked his cock in and out of her mouth, taking as much as she could manage each time.

His breathing became harsh and uneven, his groans more abandoned. Ellie savored every carnal sound as he started to guide her to a faster pace.

Finally, he pulled her mouth away from him, grasping her gently by her hair. "Fuck, no! I'm not coming in your mouth right now. It's not what either one of us needs." He grabbed her hands and pulled. "Ride me, Ellie. I need to feel your body against mine. I need to feel you come around my cock. I've wanted it for days."

She wanted that, too, but... "I don't want to hurt you." Cautiously, she straddled his lap.

God, he felt good. He smelled good.

"If you don't fuck me, you're going to kill me," he said, his voice graveled with frustration. "Kiss me," he insisted bossily.

She let her arms rest on his shoulders and her hands land on the back of the sofa as she leaned down gently and gave him a tender kiss on the lips before she looked into his tumultuous eyes and told him in little more than a whisper, "I love you, Zane Colter. No more second-guessing how I feel. I never want to have any regrets when it comes to you. If something had happened and I'd never told you, I couldn't have lived with myself."

He slid his arms around her body, moving his hand soothingly over her ass and up her back. "If something happens to you, I don't think I'd want to live at all," Zane confessed. "I regretted it, Ellie. When I thought that Sean was going to off me, my only regret was that I never told you exactly how I felt about you."

His hand stroked up her neck, and he pulled her mouth down to his. The embrace was tender and demanding, sweet and hot.

She moaned and her hips moved, rubbing against his cock in an unconscious motion, something she couldn't stop if she wanted to. Ellie wanted to climb inside him and never leave.

When his mouth slid down her neck, taking little nips of her skin before soothing them with his tongue, he murmured hoarsely against her throat, "Now fuck me before I lose my mind."

Ellie shifted, using one of her hands to guide him to her before she sunk down on him as gently as possible. "Easy," she cautioned.

"Baby, I don't think there's any way to avoid making this a rough ride." Grasping her hips, Zane pushed up and sank deeper inside her. "Oh, hell, yeah," he groaned. "You feel so damn perfect. So tight, so damn hot, Ellie. You're mine. I think you were always meant to be mine."

Gasping as he bucked up again, Ellie slapped her hands on his shoulders for support, moaning as he ducked his head and took one of her nipples into his mouth. His teeth, lips, and tongue teased her breasts as his hands guided her to a frantic up and down rhythm that was driving her crazy.

"Tell me you love me now," Zane growled as he slammed up into her again and again. "Tell me you're mine. Tell me you need me as much as I need you."

Breathless with pleasure, she answered, "I love you. I need you. I'll always be yours, and you'll always be mine."

Ellie was feeling the same possessive, covetous emotions that Zane was experiencing right now, and she lost herself to the carnal ecstasy that was coursing through her body.

Her orgasm wasn't just approaching; it was racing toward her like a speeding train. Her short nails dug into his shoulders, and she leaned her head back. The shift of position made his cock slide along her throbbing clit, and, unable to take any more, Ellie let her climax rock her body, the muscular walls of her channel squeezing down on Zane's pummeling cock.

"Fuck, baby. Come for me," Zane demanded. "Jesus, Ellie, I love you. I love you so damn much!"

The bliss of what was happening to her body and the thrill of hearing Zane's expression of love while he was moving inside her was probably the most satisfying, hottest experience she'd ever known. When he wrapped his hand around her neck and pulled her down to take her mouth greedily, Ellie rode out the prolonged climax, knowing Zane was about to spill himself deep inside her.

He broke off the ferocious embrace and put his head back, grabbed her ass and let his fiery release consume him, sending Ellie up in flames and taking her with him.

Chapter 20

Ellie moved from Zane's lap as soon as she caught her breath. "I thought I told you *not* to move."

Zane's spontaneous, deep laugh boomed through the family room. "Did you really expect that to happen?"

"Yes," she answered, feeling a little naïve. "You could have just laid there and enjoyed it."

He pulled her naked body against his and put his arm around her, letting her rest her head against his shoulder. "Never going to happen, sweetheart."

"Why?"

"Because I want you too much not to be a willing participant."

He more than just participated. He liked to be in control. Maybe it was because she'd initially been a virgin, but she was pretty sure it was just his nature. "Are you feeling okay?" she asked anxiously. It had been a rough and tumble session, and he wasn't completely recovered.

"No. You wrecked me," he complained good-naturedly.

Ellie smiled, knowing he was just fine by the tone of his voice. "How are you feeling about what happened with Sean?" The top guy in his lab had betrayed him. That had to hurt.

"I wanted to kill him. But when I think of what I have, I can't be bitter. I wish I would have seen the signs, but there weren't any huge red flags. The whole thing is kind of surreal, actually."

Ellie nodded against his shoulder. "I think so, too. I'm so sorry he hurt you." She meant both physically and emotionally.

"Honestly, I don't give a shit anymore. His ass will rot in jail and we'll be happy. Although we really need to talk about you putting your life in danger."

"No, we don't. There's nothing I wouldn't do for you," she answered haughtily. "End of discussion."

"That was pretty short," Zane teased, playing with a lock of her hair.

"You know you would have done the same thing."

"Granted," he admitted. "But Tate and Marcus should have left you and Lara out of the whole thing."

She looked up at him with a glare. "Why? Just because we're women?"

"Not at all. Just because I don't think Tate or I could live without the women we love. It would have killed me if Sean had hurt you, Ell. I know Tate feels the same. I don't know how Lara convinced him to let her go."

"I think they worked out a deal. Her involvement was to be limited. She was an FBI agent, so she knows how to use a gun, and can kick some major ass. I think she insisted, and Tate had no choice but to either make the situation controlled or risk her doing as she pleased. She wanted to help. That's the way Lara is. She couldn't sit back and wait while she had the skills to be backup."

"I suppose," he agreed reluctantly. "It's not that I'm not grateful to be alive, but I didn't want to see anybody I cared about hurt because of me."

Ellie gently stroked his neck. "The only one hurt was you."

"I'll live," he joked. "I'm nearly healed."

"I hope you're planning on giving yourself time to recover before you jump back into the lab."

"My assistant director has taken over Sean's position. I don't plan on hurrying back. They can manage just fine without me for a while."

"Do you want me to go back to Denver and see what I can do to help the new guy since Elena is gone?" Ellie didn't want to leave Zane, but it was better than him hurrying back to work.

"Hell, no," Zane objected fiercely. "In fact, I've been thinking about firing you."

"What?" She lifted her head to look at him. "Why? I organized you; I keep you on track. I've done a damn good job."

"Agreed." He planted a gentle kiss on her forehead. "But your business is picking up, and I want you to pursue your own dreams, Ell. I'll help you, and you help me stay organized from home so you can start to grow your company. The only thing stopping you is time. You're too damn busy when you have to go to the office every day."

"Zane, I still need a job. I have to support myself while I'm trying to build a business."

"No, you don't." He got up and went to retrieve his jeans, fumbling through his pocket until he pulled out what he wanted.

Ellie watched him curiously, wondering what he was doing.

He turned, and came back to the couch and kneeled beside her. "This isn't the way I planned this. I thought of all kinds of romantic ways to do it, but now feels like the right time even though we are both naked and sweaty."

He grinned at her and her heart melted as he popped open a jewelry box holding an enormous diamond. When it finally dawned on Ellie exactly what he was doing, her heart skittered.

"Marry me, Ellie. Please. I'll never be worth a damn without you, and I promise to always love you, and be the best man I can be for you."

Zane couldn't ever be a better man than he already was, and her tears started to flow as she looked at the glittery diamond ring nestled in velvet, another gorgeous Mia Hamilton creation. She tried to speak, but the words wouldn't come.

"Don't say no," Zane said hastily when she didn't answer. "If you need some time to decide, that's okay. But don't say no."

She reached out and touched the beautiful ring carefully, tracing the center stone and the accent diamonds surrounding it. "It's beautiful. I want to say yes."

"Then fucking say it," Zane grumbled, not guarding his words because he was obviously anxious.

Ellie squashed her old hang-ups about not being good enough for a man like Zane, or that he couldn't possibly really love her.

He did love her.

And nobody would ever love him and cherish his love like Ellie would.

She realized the only one holding her back from making her dreams come true was herself.

"Yes," she answered with a happy sob. "Yes. Yes. Yes."

He pulled the ring from the box and slipped it onto her finger. "You hesitated," he pointed out carefully.

"Old ghosts," she confessed. "But I think I exorcised them."

He nodded like he understood, which he probably did. She and Zane sensed each other's emotions at times, in an almost unbelievable kind of way.

"There's nothing I want more than to be your wife." Ellie hauled him onto the couch and kissed him with all of the love and joy that she was feeling at the moment.

He cuddled her against him when they finally had to come up for air. "Let me help you build your business, Ellie. My lab is *my* dream. I want you to reach for your own, too."

In many ways, *Zane* was her real dream. But she did desperately want her business, too. "Some businesses fail," she reminded him.

"Ellie, you'll have some of the greatest business minds in existence to mentor you along. Including me. I might be a science geek, but my lab makes a more than healthy profit. Then there's Marcus, Gabe, and Chloe, and a whole lot of other friends who are amazingly successful in business to give you any advice you need."

"I'm still going to try to organize you," she warned him.

"That's okay. It's your strength, and I need that. Hopefully you'll need some of my strengths, too."

Ellie smiled at him through her tears. There was never any mention of the fact that it didn't matter whether or not her business failed because he was filthy rich. He had faith in her, and didn't make light of what she wanted for herself. "I need all of you," Ellie whispered, her voice trembling with emotion.

"You have me," he answered gruffly. "Now that you said yes and my ring is on your finger, you're officially stuck with me."

She nodded with a smile on her face. "I think I can handle that."

He kissed her with so much tenderness and adoration that she sighed happily when he finally ended the magical meeting of lips that was an act of love.

Ellie cuddled into Zane, feeling a sense of security that was completely new to her, especially after what she'd endured. She was used to being alone, taking care of herself. Until Zane had rescued her, showed her how it felt to give and receive real love.

Her insecurities and her struggles were in the past. Zane was now her future.

For once in her life, Ellie fell asleep unconcerned about what tomorrow would bring. Now that she had Zane beside her, Ellie would have the one thing she'd always wanted. She'd know that no matter what the future held for her, she'd always be loved.

Epilogue

Six Months Later...

As Blake Colter watched Ellie pledge her life to Zane's, he was feeling restless. Not that he wasn't happy for Zane—because he *was* glad his younger brother had found the woman he wanted for the rest of his life. Ellie and Zane deserved every bit of happiness that they were experiencing right now.

Ellie looked beautiful, her blonde hair upswept and her face glowing with love for her groom. Chloe was standing beside her, looking elegant in her matron of honor gown. Marcus was beside Zane, standing as his best man.

Blake couldn't imagine what it would be like to willingly commit himself to another person completely, like Tate and Chloe had done, and Zane was doing right now. With his political ambitions a priority, it left very little room in his life for a relationship, even if he could find a woman who wasn't impressed by him being a senator and a billionaire.

When he was home, he had to attend to ranch business. When he was in DC, he had a job to do. Although those two things were good excuses, Blake knew the biggest reason he wasn't seriously involved with a woman was because he hadn't found one that he couldn't live without.

Women used him because he had money and some political power. He used them for sex.

Truth was, he hadn't even found a woman who looked at him like Chloe looked at Gabe, or like Zane looked at Ellie.

Blake looked at Ellie and then at Chloe, both of them looking radiant and happy. Just like when they were kids, the two best friends were often together, and now they'd brought Lara into their circle. The three of them had gotten very involved with Asha's Fund. He found it pretty amazing that two women who'd been so damaged were now helping other women to escape from the hell they'd both been through, and Lara, with her psychology background, rounded out the threesome of friends perfectly.

The ceremony was over quickly, and everyone followed the wedding party to the reception, which just so happened to be in the same place: their mother's resort.

Aileen Colter had been delighted when she'd heard Ellie and Zane were getting married, and she'd fussed over every detail since Ellie's mom hadn't been around for the planning stages.

Everybody flowed from the large hall and into the ballroom easily. Blake followed the crowd, hoping he could get something to eat. He'd gotten in late last night, and he was starving.

Before he could go fill a plate with food, Marcus approached him and nodded for Blake to meet him outside. He exited onto the balcony, Marcus right behind him.

Blake's twin didn't mess around with the niceties. He got right to the point. "You know how I asked you if I needed a favor if you would do it?"

"Yeah," Blake answered cautiously.

"I need that favor."

"Now?" Blake asked grumpily. Hell, he'd just gotten back home, just gotten a break from Congress.

"I'm sorry. I know it's shitty timing, but lives are at stake right now," Marcus answered grimly.

"Are you planning on telling me what this is all about?" If he was going to help, Marcus couldn't keep him totally in the dark.

"Some," Marcus agreed. "But only what you need to know."

Blake shook his head. "Everything. Marcus, I know something is up. I've sensed it for a while now. Come clean with me. This isn't just about the CIA stuff."

"No. It has nothing to do with that. Look, I *want* to tell you, but it's an election year for you, and I know you'd never lie. It might be better if you didn't know too much. Then you could honestly claim you didn't know."

"Didn't know what? If I'm going to help you, I need details."

Marcus paced the small patio, his expression grave. "I'll tell you, if that's what it's going to take to get your help."

Blake listened while Marcus started explaining. To say he was surprised at what he *didn't* know about his twin was an understatement. Marcus led an entire portion of his life that not a single one of the Colter family even knew about.

When had he lost track of his twin brother and exactly what was going on in his life? They used to share everything.

"Why didn't you tell me before?"

"Because I gave my word that I wouldn't."

"Your plan will never work."

"It has to," Marcus countered. "The consequences of failing are not an option."

His brother was right. If the plan failed, lives could be lost.

"You two need to come in and eat," Aileen Colter directed them from the doorway of the patio. "Now," she insisted. "You both just got in last night. You have to be hungry."

Blake and Marcus exchanged a silent communication as they started to leave the patio. "We're on our way," Blake said loudly enough for his mother to hear. In a softer tone, he said to Marcus, "We need to talk about this later."

"We'll get together at my place when the reception is over," Marcus agreed.

"Actually, I am hungry," Blake confessed.

"Me, too. And we have a bride and groom to celebrate with. I didn't think Zane would ever get married."

"He's happy," Blake informed his brother as they stepped back into the ballroom.

"So is Ellie."

He and Marcus started filling their plates once they hit the buffet table. Blake drifted away from his twin in the large crowd, but it didn't matter. He'd see him later that night, and when he did, Blake still had plenty of questions for him. He knew he'd help Marcus, but he wasn't going into anything blind. Before the evening ended, he'd get the answers he needed from his twin to play the very dangerous game Marcus was planning.

~The End~

Please visit me at:
http://www.authorjsscott.com
http://www.facebook.com/authorjsscott

You can write to me at
jsscott_author@hotmail.com

You can also tweet
@AuthorJSScott

Please sign up for my Newsletter for updates,
new releases and exclusive excerpts.

Books by J. S. Scott:

Billionaire Obsession Series

The Billionaire's Obsession~Simon
Heart of the Billionaire
The Billionaire's Salvation
The Billionaire's Game
Billionaire Undone~Travis
Billionaire Unmasked~Jason
Billionaire Untamed~Tate
Billionaire Unbound~Chloe
Billionaire Undaunted~Zane
Billionaire Unknown~Blake
Billionaire Unveiled~Marcus
Billionaire Unloved~Jett
Billionaire Unwed~Zeke
Billionaire Unchallenged~Carter
Billionaire Unattainable~Mason

Billionaire Undercover~Hudson
Billionaire Unexpected~Jax
Billionaire Unnoticed~Cooper
Billionaire Unclaimed~Chase

British Billionaires Series

Tell Me You're Mine
Tell Me I'm Yours
Tell Me This Is Forever

Sinclair Series

The Billionaire's Christmas
No Ordinary Billionaire
The Forbidden Billionaire
The Billionaire's Touch
The Billionaire's Voice
The Billionaire Takes All
The Billionaire's Secret
Only A Millionaire

Accidental Billionaires

Ensnared
Entangled
Enamored
Enchanted
Endeared

Walker Brothers Series

Release
Player
Damaged

The Sentinel Demons

The Sentinel Demons: The Complete Collection
A Dangerous Bargain
A Dangerous Hunger
A Dangerous Fury
A Dangerous Demon King

The Vampire Coalition Series

The Vampire Coalition: The Complete Collection
The Rough Mating of a Vampire (Prelude)
Ethan's Mate
Rory's Mate
Nathan's Mate
Liam's Mate
Daric's Mate

Changeling Encounters Series

Changeling Encounters: The Complete Collection
Mate Of The Werewolf
The Dangers Of Adopting A Werewolf
All I Want For Christmas Is A Werewolf

The Pleasures of His Punishment

The Pleasures of His Punishment: The Complete Collection
The Billionaire Next Door
The Millionaire and the Librarian
Riding with the Cop
Secret Desires of the Counselor
In Trouble with the Boss
Rough Ride with a Cowboy
Rough Day for the Teacher
A Forfeit for a Cowboy

Just what the Doctor Ordered
Wicked Romance of a Vampire

The Curve Collection: Big Girls and Bad Boys Series

The Curve Collection: The Complete Collection
The Curve Ball
The Beast Loves Curves
Curves by Design

Writing as Lane Parker

Dearest Stalker: Part 1
Dearest Stalker: A Complete Collection
A Christmas Dream
A Valentine's Dream
Lost: A Mountain Man Rescue Romance

A Dark Horse Novel w/ Cali MacKay

Bound
Hacked

Taken By A Trillionaire Series

Virgin for the Trillionaire by Ruth Cardello
Virgin for the Prince by J.S. Scott
Virgin to Conquer by Melody Anne
Prince Bryan: Taken By A Trillionaire

Other Titles

Well Played w/Ruth Cardello

Printed in Great Britain
by Amazon

46742009R00118